THE GOOD DEITY

BOOK ONE
ALMOST COUNTABLE

OUTLANDERS OF THE MULTIVERSE
COLLECTION

BY D.N. LEO

Narrative Land Publishing
Narrativeland.com

Get D.N. Leo's exclusive library FOR FREE

**The library contains 4 books
including e-books, audiobooks and a lot more exclusive
content**

Details can be found at http://dnleo.com

THE GOOD DEITY

By D.N. Leo

Almost Countable
Almost Sure
Almost Everywhere

More information can be found at
http://dnleo.com

The Good Deity - Almost Sure - Book 2
By D.N. Leo

http://dnleo.com

Synopsis

Mya Portman is a young deity who believes she can tell the difference between good and evil. She is confident that she can save one thousand innocent souls from an unnatural death, and she has bet her freedom on it. A thousand years later, she is still working off the debts.

Now she is given an opportunity to pay off her debts. The only condition is that, for once, she has to turn a blind eye on some cases and allow people to die. Her record suggests that she will fail to look away again. But this time, it isn't just an opportunity to pay off her debt, it might be her Goddess's ultimatum.

This second installment in an urban fantasy, supernatural suspense series, filled with twists and turns, will make you question what you take for granted in this modern world.

PART ONE

CHAPTER 1

The theater exploded with a standing ovation. From under the bright spotlight on the stage of the famous Sydney Opera House, she smiled at the audience. They obviously admired her. She wondered whether it was the allure of the limelight that made these people applaud whoever stood on the stage, playing the lead role in a famous play, or whether they truly prized her talent as a performer. She doubted it was the latter.

Other cast members had joined her on the stage to say goodbye to the night's audience. Although *The Woman in the Asylum* had been one of the most successful and longest-running shows, no one knew what would happen with the next performance. It was the nature of the trade. The political and cultural landscape on this planet had changed so swiftly in the last decade. Everyone knew they should feel fortunate for what they'd been able to enjoy up to this point.

The curtain finally closed, irrespective of the amount of applause they had received.

She turned to go to her changing room.

"Casey," a voice called from behind.

"Yes, Richard," she answered without looking back. Richard was her talent manager and the director of the theater company. He was also the only one who called her by her first name.

He approached her. Under the dim lights of the backstage, he looked quite attractive. He was in his mid-fifties but could have passed for forty. Formidable, tall, and authoritative with a deep voice, Casey thought he'd have made a good performer. But he'd chosen business over art.

"This is our last show here. People would appreciate it if you gave the interview in your costume."

She smiled. "By people, I take it you mean the press?"

He smiled back. "No, the press isn't important. Your fans are."

"Indeed. They pay our bills." She nodded. "All right." She gestured up and down her body. "I'll hang around in this *very comfortable* outfit for a little longer." The last scene had been a war scene, and she was attired in armor not designed for comfort. She frowned. "What else, Richard? What's bothering you?"

He paused then shook his head. "Nothing." He chuckled. "It's nothing...it's silly," he muttered mostly to himself and turned to walk away.

"You're worried about it, aren't you?" she asked at his back.

Richard turned around. "About what?"

She approached him and touched his lapel. "The myth. Next week is the birthday of this theatrical company. And not only a birthday. It's a centenary."

"It was before our time, Casey. Plus, as you said, it's a myth."

"So did you think making me stay in this stage armor would somehow protect me?"

"Are you insane?"

"It's not the press. It's not the fans. I saw you ordering the records of the company and truckloads of books about its history last week. Did you just suddenly have an urge to find out what happens to this company every hundred years?"

Richard whirled around. "That's ridiculous, Casey."

"Really?" She raised an eyebrow. "All right. I'll take this off then." She tugged at her breastplate.

"Okay, I give up. Yes, you can take that costume off. But can you please be careful?"

"Careful of what? Dying a violent death?"

"It might be a myth, but it's not a joke. What happened before happened to lead performers." He narrowed his eyes. "So you knew this, and you still joined the company? You joined before me."

"I didn't know anything before this. I saw you digging for info last week, so I sneaked in and read the stuff in your office."

He nodded. "So you don't believe it. You think it's a myth. Every hundred years, there have been accidents. Lead cast members have died tragic deaths. No one noticed because of the large interval between them."

"Why did you notice?"

"I just had a hunch."

She laughed. "You should never do serious business on a hunch."

He shook his head. "It was really a feeling. I don't know. I've just sensed some unusual, dark, and spooky aura around the place in the last few weeks. I'm not superstitious. But it just felt as if the place was haunted."

She smiled. "Might be you're reading too much into the current play."

He nodded. "Maybe. But the play has been performed for a long time. The spooky aura has been here for only a few weeks. Why now?"

She shrugged. "I didn't know you were that sensitive to the ambiance of the theater."

"It's not the ambiance, Casey. It's the aura..."

She looked up, and from behind him and above, she swore she saw a shadow. A string of rope suddenly broke loose and hung down, and a stage light rail slid out of place slightly. She knew the rope was going to snap, and the steel rail would then drop down behind Richard. If she pushed him out of the way, she would be the one copping the hit. But if she didn't, it would be his head that sustained the impact.

CHAPTER 2

Leon opened his eyes and found himself unable to move any part of his body. But he could feel the blood running through his veins, and his heart was still beating. He was alive—just not quite as lively as he'd like. He had been paralyzed as soon as the gigantic black cat bit him.

He recalled the incident in the woods now. Zach had gone after Mya. He had been talking to Kirra, using his limited amount of English to try to get to know her better. He knew Zach would get Mya back, and then they would go to Eudaiz together. Eudaiz was the universe in which Zach was residing.

That would mean Leon would have to leave Kirra behind. She was human and had nothing to do with any other world other than this current one she lived in. He felt a pang of unusual sensation just thinking about the fact that he might never see her again.

He wasn't an idiot. He knew he shouldn't think about her—a human in another world—especially when he knew nothing about her. He made a mental note to ask Mya later about human courting rituals.

He tried to move again but couldn't. It was strange that a bite from a cat could have such an effect. Usually, only poisonous snakes or scorpions would have venom poisonous enough to immobilize him. He was the head of the temple guard at the Babylonian court, for the Goddess's sake. He'd give his body a bit more time to dissolve the poison before trying something else.

He heard footsteps above him and figured he must be lying in a basement of some kind. He tried to turn his head to the side to survey the area and found his neck had loosened up a bit. The footsteps above weren't random but in rhythm, as if several people were dancing. The faint sounds of a musical instrument found its way to the basement. He squinted into the darkness and saw a line of light as if the floor had a crack which ran into a corner.

He heard laughter and maybe singing. He recognized the language. It was English. Similar to what Mya spoke. He tried to inch his shoulders up and found that his right shoulder moved. He smiled and tried his legs.

A beam of light poured in from a far corner as if someone had pushed the door in for a few seconds and then slammed it closed. A male and female voice murmured something. They laughed. She giggled, and it sounded as if they were kissing. He heard the sound of fabric tearing, and then the woman moaned in pleasure.

"Are you sure it's going to work? He was supposed to announce it now," the man said.

"Yes, of course it'll work. Have I ever failed in any of your plans?"

"No. You're very resourceful."

"Is that all?"

"And smart. And beautiful..."

The woman chuckled. "And what do I get for having all of those good qualities?"

"Anything you want. I promised you half of the company. What else do you want?"

Silence.

"Come on, honey, don't give me that look. I'm married."

"For money!"

"Yes, but I still need that money. Can you be a bit more patient? Richard will announce his resignation. He'll go away with that silly actress. And the rest will be history."

Leon wriggled his body hard to see how much movement he'd regained. He tried to clear his throat to see if he could make a sound. He could feel it—his voice was coming back to him.

Then he felt a puff of hot air blowing into his face. He turned and saw the face of the black cat right next to him. Its eyes glowed green, and its teeth were bared. Its lips rubbed right against his face. And if he wasn't mistaken, he heard it growl in Babylonian, "Hush, or be dead."

Leon tried harder to move, inching his body away from the cat. *Silent, my backside!* he thought. *I'd rather be dead than feeling your disgusting breath blowing into my face!*

His legs moved an inch or so.

His voice came back.

He shouted for help. But before the sound escaped his throat, the cat sank its teeth into his shoulder. He blacked out again.

CHAPTER 3

Mya felt a warm sensation wash over her when Zach embraced her from behind. He whispered into her ear. "You're brooding, my deity. Don't worry about the jar or the potion. We'll get it and bring it to the Goddess. We'll pay off all of your debts. You'll never ever have to think about Ishtar again."

She turned and looked at him. There was no natural sunlight in the room because she had closed the door and all the windows in their cabin at the campsite to avoid any unwelcome animal guests. Under the dim light of the table lamp, she could still see Zach's soft green eyes. They always warmed a shade whenever he looked at her, even before they had been in a relationship. He didn't even try to hide it. He must know the effect of that look on the female species. She could only hope he didn't use it on every female he came across.

She played with a strand of his dark brown hair. "How are you feeling?" she asked.

"Not a hundred percent..."

She frowned. "Get more rest then. We can't go anywhere if you're not a hundred percent." She silently cursed the female lynx Elanora. The nasty, sadistic woman had peered into Zach's mind, read his fatal point, pointed the gun at her to distract Zach, and attacked him where he was most vulnerable.

Well, not right at the point below his shoulder on his back, but close enough. Mya shuddered. If Elanora had meant to kill Zach, he would have been dead.

He kissed her on the lips and then gently eased away. "Let's go."

"No, I'll go find Leon. You stay here until you're a hundred percent again."

He chuckled. "Why would you want me to deteriorate?"

"What are you talking about, Zach?"

"I'm at a hundred and *fifty* percent capacity." He grinned.

She punched his chest. "Then let's go." She scrambled up, but he pulled her back down into his arms.

"Calm down, my deity. You can't do anything good in the state you're in now."

"What state?" she said, on the verge of switching on her deity vision to check on Leon. She had refrained from doing so because Zach wasn't in any condition to be left alone, and if she found out Leon needed help, there would be nothing she could do. "Where's Kirra?" She spat out the question for no particular reason. It was just there, in the middle of her thought process for some reason. Well, it wasn't much of a process, but at least it was something.

"Your mind is clogging up again, Mya. It happens whenever you panic."

She pushed at him. "Don't talk like you know me so well. Not long ago, you were still calling me Professor Portman."

"And which part of that title isn't correct?"

"The part—"

He interrupted her speech by kissing her until she melted in his arms.

"There. You're calm now," he said. "I know you're worried about Leon. But he's fine." He glanced at his wrist unit. "And I know you want to switch on your deity mode so you can check on him. But I don't want you to do that—I don't like the look on your face when you're in deity mode. It weirds me out." He tapped his finger on the screen of his wrist unit. "The unit suggests that Leon's vitals are healthy. Meaning he's alive and well. Not only that, I know his location."

She narrowed her eyes. "Why didn't you say so?"

"You didn't ask. Plus, I was busy kissing you." He grinned again.

"How can you be so sure he's fine? How can your unit tell? Is it psychic?"

Zach chuckled. "One psychic in this room is enough. I gave him some of my eudqi and appointed him as my successor, remember? So I got a sample of his blood and entered his data into the system. They track him, of course."

She scrambled out of the bed. "You track him because eudqi is such an important energy source to Eudaiz. If anything happens to Leon, you don't want your adversaries to sample the substance. You'd have to kill him—or so you've said."

Zach stood up. "Yes, there's that. But I do care for Leon. He's my successor, Mya."

"Really? So if you find Leon, and his blood or the eudqi has been taken, would you kill him?"

"If it's already been taken, what good would it do to kill him? If I did have to kill him, it would be before the eudqi was taken. But that's beside the point. There are many ways to take this. Why do you have to take it the wrong way?"

Mya waved her arms in the air. "I don't know." She whirled around. Something wasn't right. Something was ticking her off. *Calm down,* she told herself.

Zach grabbed at her shoulders. "Mya, listen to me. You're agitated and snappish. What's happening?"

"I don't know. This...only happens when..." She looked at him. "Oh no... It happens when someone I'm supposed to save is on my list, but I couldn't get to my vision to check..."

Zach blew out a breath. "Okay, then check. I really do hate to see you with those blank eyes, but I would rather see that than you whirling around not knowing what to do."

"What if it's Leon? What if it's Leon that I have to save, but it's too late because I'm here!"

"I told you he's fine. Alive. If he's now on your list to save, that's great because we're going to go and get him anyway. You, he, and I will go back to Eudaiz. Everything will be fine." He approached and held her shoulders. "Now let's check so that you can be sure and calm down." He smiled at her.

She nodded and was just about to switch on her deity vision.

"Knock knock!" Kirra's voice interrupted from outside the room.

Mya stopped and looked up at Zach. He gazed into her eyes. He knew her rather well now, and she didn't need to explain.

"It's Kirra. She triggered your anxiety, didn't she?" Zach asked.

"I'm afraid so." She hadn't had a chance to check her vision, but as soon as the name came into her mind, her agitation eased. That was a sign that she had gotten to the right subject, the one who needed her attention. All she had to do now was to switch on the vision to find out the cause of death.

"Trouble," Mya muttered.

"If she's on the list of people you must save, then we will save her. How is this any different from the thousands of other lives you have saved over the years?"

"There are *two* lists. I'm supposed to save those on one of the lists, but I'm not allowed to save the people on the destined-to-die list. That's part of the fine print in the Goddess's agreement."

"Sadistic b—"

"Shhh, you shouldn't curse the Goddess."

"I don't belong to the world she rules."

"Still, it's not helpful, Zach."

He nodded and sat down on the bed. "Let's find out which list Kirra is on then."

Mya switched on her deity vision.

The image hit her mind like a storm from hell—a sword pierced Kirra's heart, and her body floated and spun in a whirlwind of fire.

Mya's knees buckled. She switched back to her human vision and found Zach holding her. Tears rolled down her face. She shuddered then regained her footing. She could feel all the muscles in Zach's body quivering. He had somehow connected with her emotion. He released her and brushed a strand of hair from her forehead.

"It was bad, wasn't it?"

She nodded. "I've never seen images before, just text. I'd get the information about the possible cause of death and the list the subject was on. But this time...all I saw was an image of Kirra. I don't know which list she's on."

"What did you see?"

"She was on fire...floating. And a sword pierced her heart."

"Anybody home?" Kirra's voice drifted in again.

Zach opened the door to see Kirra standing outside with a smile as bright as the sunshine on her face.

CHAPTER 4

From the floor, Richard looked at Casey. He saw the reflection of the falling steel rail behind him in her eyes. Without thinking, he pushed her out of the way. It was strange, though. He thought she resisted his push. She saw the falling rail. But from his perspective, it was only a reflection in her eyes. Why would she want to stand in the way? But maybe it was his imagination. It was dark. He felt it hit him from behind and then the impact of his body as it hit the concrete floor. Then his world went completely dark.

One light stroke cut across the darkness. Another one. Then there was sound. He could hear people murmuring. He opened his eyes and realized he was in an emergency room. The concerned face of a nurse hovered above his own.

"How are you feeling?" she asked while simultaneously checking the tubes connected to his arm and the monitor next to his bed.

"How's Casey?"

The nurse turned to look at him. He knew it was irrational to assume she knew who Casey was, but a strange nervousness stabbed at him, and he couldn't think straight. Maybe Casey was famous enough that people would recognize her name.

"You have a mild concussion, Mr. Lane. But Ms. Anderson wasn't that lucky."

He sat up, but the nurse pushed him back down. "She's in the critical unit. You can't visit her, sir."

He flopped back down, recalling pushing her out of the way of way of the falling rail. "How could her injury be that bad when I only have a mild concussion?"

"What injury?" the nurse asked.

"The falling rail. It hit me. It must have hit her. I mustn't have been quick enough..."

The nurse looked puzzled. "You need to lie down. I'll go and get the doctor."

"No. Tell me what happened to Casey."

"She had a heart attack. There were no other injuries the doctor diagnosed when you both arrived."

"A heart attack? What about the rail? I mean—"

"What rail, Mr. Lane? Are you saying Ms. Anderson has other injuries we should check on? There's nothing but a critical heart attack on her chart. Which is strange because the doctor said she has no history of a heart condition."

"I need to see her."

"All right. I'll get the doctor. If he clears you, I'll take you to Ms. Anderson."

Richard nodded and sat back down while the nurse scurried out of the room. As soon as she turned the corner, he scrambled out of bed and scooted out the door. He followed the signs and made his way to the intensive care unit. In the room, Casey lay lifelessly on a bed.

He approached the bed, feeling helpless. He and Casey had only a professional relationship, but they had worked together for a long time, and he understandably had feelings for her.

He wasn't sure if she had any feelings for him.

He heard a low growl behind him. Before he could turn around, he was picked up, and his face was shoved into a wall. He could feel the heat from the person behind him—it had to be a large and very strong man. A male voice with a faint accent growled, "So it was you."

Richard tried without success to get out of his grasp and pull his face away from the wall.

"She hangs around because of you."

Richard shrugged harder, managing to turn around and shove the man away. "You make it sound like the fact she's lying there half dead is a good thing." Richard pointed to her lifeless body. "If her lingering around like this is what you want, shouldn't you be thanking me? Who the hell are you anyway?"

Richard looked the man up and down. Tall, strong, in his thirties. He had some resemblance to Casey. What that resemblance was, he couldn't tell. But while it always felt to him as if Casey had a rainbow of light around her, this man was surrounded by a dark aura.

The man glanced briefly at Richard then turned toward Casey's bed. He started pulling out the tubes and other devices monitoring her vitals.

"Hey, what do you think you're doing?" Richard grabbed the man's shoulder in an attempt to stop him from disturbing Casey. His shoulder didn't budge an inch—he was incredibly strong. He glared at Richard and continued to do what he was doing.

Footsteps and the sound of medical staff rushing along the corridor echoed into the room. Richard pushed the man, but he swung his arm and flung Richard across the room. When the man had freed Casey from the tubes and needles, he picked her up and began to carry her out.

"Goddamn it!" Richard cursed and grabbed a chair from the corner of the room. Using all of his strength, he swung the chair at the man's head from behind. The chair broke on impact. The man stumbled, turned, and dropped Casey back onto the bed.

When the man turned back around to face Richard, his eyes were bloodshot. Richard could tell he was hurt. He approached Richard slowly. Richard was tall, but the man was at least six foot six, and there were rock hard muscles rippling under those clothes. If he tried to land a punch on him, Richard didn't think he'd leave any bones unbroken in his hand. But still he clung to the remnants of the broken chair and stood his ground, his body pressed right up against the man.

Richard swung a piece of the chair at him, but the man caught it midair. "She traded a life for you," the man growled, "but don't think I wouldn't kill you."

Richard yanked the piece of wood out of the man's grip. "What the fuck do you mean by that?"

The man turned toward Casey. "I have to take her away."

Richard stomped a kick at the man's back. He stumbled again and turned around.

"Attack me one more time, and I'll break every bone in your body."

"Then come here and do it. I can't let you take Casey. You have to let the doctors do their work or she'll die."

A doctor and two nurses rushed into the room and registered the situation. One of the nurses ran back out to call security. The man looked at Casey again. Richard saw nothing different, but the man seemed to panic. "No, don't go." He rushed toward the bed and grabbed Casey's hand.

When he wasn't paying attention, the doctor jabbed a needle into his neck. He staggered, the drug seeming to have a significant effect on him. He swayed. Then he turned around, kicked out the window, and jumped out.

The doctor and the nurse hurried toward Casey's bed. In front of everyone's astonished eyes, Casey's body glowed and then disintegrated into thousands of shiny particles which soon vanished into nothing.

Richard leaned against the wall as he observed what happened. The world was a blur, and then it turned into darkness. When his mind was floating, he thought he heard Casey's voice. There was an insistent echoing sound within a muddle of other noises, but her exquisite voice was the one thing he could never mistake for anything else in this world.

She sang to him. It was the song she had sung in her audition to join the company and take the lead role. There was one thing he had never told her—when he was considering becoming a part of this theatrical company, management had shown him the artists' portfolios as their asset. He had watched their audition tapes, and as soon as he'd heard her voice, he made the decision to join the company.

He should have told her that before. Now she was gone. And he was sinking into a dark place.

CHAPTER 5

Leon flexed his muscles and found he was able to move. It felt good. The talking black cat had been gone for a long time, enough for him to gain his strength back. He sat up and looked around. He was definitely in the dungeon of a castle. No, they wouldn't call it a castle in this world. Mya referred to these venues as buildings, or sometimes premises. Anyway, he couldn't care less—he had to get out of here.

In not too long, Leon's body was completely mobile. He stood up and took in the scene. Around him were several black boxes the size of the small table where he sat to have breakfast in his private chamber. There were also gigantic boxes the size of coffins. And boxes in sizes everywhere in between. He worked his way around all of them and found a small door. Pushing it open, he stepped outside into the magnificent sunshine of a glorious day.

He looked back at the building he had just left. Although it didn't have a castle-like shape, it was just as imposing. From his vantage point, the roof of the building looked like stacks of seashells. The people around him in the street looked friendly. There were several moving vehicles that looked like horseless carriages. He had been in one of those before with Zach as he maneuvered the machine from the front seat with a round ring he called the steering wheel. Mya called these vehicles "cars." He didn't like being in a confined space and definitely didn't look forward to being inside one of those moving boxes again.

He needed to find Mya. He could transport himself back to the Babylonian court, and from there, he would be able to find out where she was and channel to her as he had done several times in the past. But going back to the court now without Mya would be an acceptance of defeat and an admittance of the failure of the mission. For that, he would have Ishtar's wrath to deal with before he would even be able to find Mya. But on this mission, he came here as a man, without any supernatural assistance from the court.

Leon shook his head. He wouldn't go back to the court now. He closed his eyes and tried to see if he could get any kind of connection to Mya. Nothing. Mya had psychic ability, but he was only the head of the temple guard—a man with fighting ability.

"Are you okay?"

Hearing a soothing female voice, he opened his eyes and saw a woman with sandy hair, about forty, looking at him with concern in her eyes. He nodded and smiled. Then he pulled out the little traveler's guide book in his pocket. He flipped to the back and opened a folded map on the last page.

"Could you tell me where I am?" he asked the woman.

She smiled. "Yes, certainly." She took the map and circled her finger around an area labeled Sydney Harbor. "You're here." She pointed at a symbol with a picture of the building that Leon recognized from the roofline. "That's the Sydney Opera House. It's very famous. You should pay it a visit."

"Thank you. I will." Leon nodded and headed in the direction of the opera house. He had come from there just a moment ago, so he knew the building and had no intention of visiting it as a tourist. But to please the kind woman who had just helped him, he kept walking. Plus, he didn't know where else to go.

He sat down on the steps in front of the Sydney Opera House. He would wait right here. He wagered Mya would use her psychic ability to find him in no time. Pulling out his guide, he turned to the "English for travelers" section and started to practice the pronunciation of some of the words he found it hard to twist his tongue around.

"Please help him."

A faint female voice brushed across his ear. Leon scrambled to his feet. The voice was gentle. Close by but echoing in to him as if from a distance. There was something in the voice that made the hair on the back of his neck stand up.

"Who's that?" he asked in Babylonian. And to his surprise, the voice repeated "Please help him" in Babylonian.

"Show yourself!" Leon commanded with his authoritative head-of-the-temple-guard tone.

The flickering image of a beautiful woman appeared in front of him in broad daylight. Her face changed from a middle-aged woman to a teen girl and then to a woman in her mid-forties.

"I don't care who you are, but I can only speak to one person at a time. Show me your true face."

"I have many faces."

"Well, just pick one and use that one to talk to me. Stop changing. You're making me dizzy." Leon glanced around quickly. It seemed that no one around him could see the image of the woman. Talking to her would make it look like he was talking to himself. He spoke between his teeth as discreetly as possible. "What's your name?"

"My identity doesn't matter. I'm not worthy of a god's notice."

Leon snorted. "Everyone is a worthy individual. And trust me, there's no god or goddess here that I can see, so don't worry. Unless— Umm, you weren't referring to me as a god, were you?"

"I was."

Leon chuckled. He wanted to laugh, but that would make him appear crazy to bystanders. "I'm not a god. I'm the head of the temple guard. I've served the Goddess for a long time. You must be seeing some sort of aura from the court."

"I can see your magical power."

Leon shook his head. If he had any magical power at all, he wouldn't be in this situation.

"Who do you want me to help? And just so you know, I don't know if I can help anyone at the moment."

"My son. He's lying at the back of this building. In plain sight. The human might hurt him. I can't help him in my current condition. No one can see or hear me except you."

Leon nodded. "I can see you certainly do have a condition! Can you stop flickering?"

"I can't."

"So your son is injured? And you want me to take him to the infirmary?"

"They don't call it an infirmary here. They call it a hospital. But I don't think he needs to go to the hospital. He just needs to be tucked away somewhere out of sight."

Leon nodded. "All right. That's easy enough. Where is he?"

"Around the corner. At the back of this building."

Leon frowned. The basement where he had been held captive was in that same corner. He walked around the building and saw a man's body sprawled face down on the steps next to the basement door. Cursing silently, he approached him. He'd have to take him into the basement, but he didn't relish the idea of running into that black cat again.

He pushed the door open and glanced inside. Leaving it open, he walked in quickly to ensure the cat wasn't there. When he didn't see it, he hurried back out, feeling a sense of relief. He turned the man over and dragged him inside.

"Thank you," the woman said.

"You're welcome."

On the ground, the man started to wake. Under the dim light of the basement, Leon stared down at him, and a rage washed through him. "It's you! You're the bloody black cat!" Leon growled.

The man's eyes sprung wide open when he saw Leon.

CHAPTER 6

Zach stared straight ahead and focused on the road. They had been driving from Wagga Wagga for a few hours and would soon arrive in Sydney. Mya was concentrating on her vision. She had been trying to use her psychic ability to connect to Leon for half an hour without success. In the back seat of the car, Kirra was absolutely quiet. Zach had had life-threatening injuries before, but he hadn't known about them in advance. He supposed he wouldn't know what to say, either, if a deity with supernatural powers told him a deadly blade was going to pierce his heart, and he was going to die.

They had discussed at length whether or not to allow Kirra to accompany them on this trip given the danger Mya had foreseen. But Kirra wanted to go. And Zach preferred to be close to her in case anything happened.

"I can't get to him," Mya said.

"I told you my wrist unit says there's a surge in his adrenaline. He might be in some sort of a fight. If so, he'd be in full alert mode. That would block your vision when you try to see into his mind."

"I'm not trying to peek into anyone's mind. I'm just trying to see if he's okay."

"Same thing."

"No, it's not."

"Mya, I'm worried, too. Let's not argue about nonsense."

"My worries aren't nonsense. But I agree. Let's not argue."

"Look out!" Kirra yelled from the backseat.

The female lynx Elanora had charged out from the nearby bush and now stood in front of them in the middle of the road. Zach was about to hit the brake, but he stopped himself. If he slammed on the brakes, the car would spin and crash. He didn't even want to think about the consequence of the impact. So instead, he aimed

41

straight at the lynx and accelerated. She jumped aside just before the car hit her.

"Smart move," Zach muttered. He slowed the car down a bit. In the rearview mirror, he could see the animal had disappeared. But in front of them, a pack of leopards marched down the road, heading right at them. Zach accelerated once again, but unlike the lynx, the leopards didn't move out of the way. It was as if they were on a suicidal mission.

The car hit the first row of leopards. The bodies of the wild animals smashed against the windshield and shattered it into thousands of pieces. The car spun and crashed into a tree at the side of the road before it could hit the second group of leopards. The car's airbags were discharged.

Zach worked his way out of the tangled airbag. "Mya! Are you okay?"

Mya was disentangling herself from her airbag as well. Her head popped up above the white fabric. "Yes," she responded.

"Kirra!" Zach called out, looking at the mess in the backseat.

Kirra pulled an airbag away from her face and muttered, "I'm fine." She reached for the buckle of her seatbelt.

"Don't unbuckle," Zach said quickly. As he spoke, they felt the impact of the animals hurling their bodies at the car. They pushed and shoved the vehicle. One of them jumped onto the hood of the car and reached its giant front paw inside. Zach pulled his dagger and stabbed at its leg. The animal roared and jumped back down off the car. It limped around on three legs, teeth bared.

"Are they the lynxes of magical leopards, Mya?" Zach asked.

"I'm not sure. But they hold a lower rank in their pack."

Zach pulled out his Eudaizian laser gun. "This gun didn't work on the old lynx we killed. But let's see if it works on these minion leopards."

He aimed at those still crashing into the car. But the gun didn't work. And it made the crazed animals even angrier.

"Great," Zach mumbled.

"They'll toss us!" Kirra shouted.

Even before she finished the sentence, the leopards pounced at their vehicle, managing to roll the car over several times. Zach kicked at the side of the car, throwing his weight in that direction as much as he could to make sure they landed on all four wheels.

"I've had enough of this," Mya growled. She unfastened her seatbelt and stepped outside the car.

"Mya!" Zach shouted, unbuckling and rushing after her. Kirra followed him.

Outside the protection of the car, they were surrounded by hundreds of menacing leopards, stealthily whirling in circles around them.

"What's your plan, Mya?" Zach asked.

"I don't have one."

"What?" Kirra exclaimed.

Zach narrowed his eyes. "Don't lie to me, Mya. What's your plan?"

The leopards approached them slowly.

"I'll tell you my plan if you kiss me."

"Mya!"

"Will you kiss me or not?"

Zach approached. He placed one hand at the nape of her neck and kissed her. She kissed him back slightly then reached her hand up and yanked his wrist unit off. She shoved him away with her other hand.

"Mya!" Zach exclaimed.

She gestured to him not to approach. They heard a low hum from the leopards. It was in sync with Mya's movement of the hand in which she was holding the wrist unit. The animals tilted their heads with each movement of her hand. It was almost as if they might start dancing if she swung her arm in a rhythm. "You see, they don't want to eat us. They're here for your wrist unit," she said.

"Even if you combine all three of us, we don't have enough meat to feed them all," Zach growled. "But I have no intention of giving them my wrist unit. Give it back to me, Mya. Elanora knows the unit wouldn't work without me anyway."

Mya tossed her chin toward the animals. "They're merely minions. They don't know that. Their task is to get this wrist unit."

"Still, I don't want to give it to them." He reached his hand out for it.

She smiled and said, "Stay here." Then she turned around and raised the unit up in the air so the animals could see. Using one of her rare abilities as a deity—running like the wind—she charged away, up the hill.

The leopards took off in her direction in a storm of fur.

Kirra ran after Mya, but Zach held her back. "No one can run as fast as she can. You'll only slow her down."

When the last leopard had left the scene, they heard a clapping sound. Elanora stepped out from behind a tree. "She must love you madly. She's trying to lure the leopards away."

Zach smiled. "She's a good deity. And very capable. You must know that by now. What can you possibly do as an alpha if you lose all of your followers?"

She chuckled. "They're not my pack. And don't try to use your charm on me. I can eat you anytime I want to. But you're not to my taste. But now...I'm going to take you. Then I'll come back for the wrist unit." She shifted into her lynx form again, shot a menacing look in Zach's direction, and charged.

Zach pushed Kirra back, pulled his daggers, and lunged at the attacking lynx.

They fought a few rounds, and Zach was sure he had done some significant damage to the animal in exchange for a few minor scratches and bite marks. Then he heard Kirra shout, "Get down, Zach!"

He flopped to the ground as the lynx leaped at him. Kirra stood next to the car with the rifle. She fired at the lynx while it was in midair. Zach's Eudaizian gun hadn't done the cat any damage, but the primitive earthly weapon in Kirra's hands did.

The animal dropped to the ground.

But in a short moment, it scrambled up, eyes blazing. Zach jumped to his feet. He could see the fire in the magical creature's eyes—the fire of fury. He wasn't sure what it could do, but he knew it would be nasty.

He looked back to where Kirra stood next to the car and saw the heat from the ground rising up like a transparent curtain of steam. A thought dawned on him, and he yelled, "Get away from the car!" He charged toward her as she ran away from the car.

Zach felt heat behind him as if someone had ignited a line of fire. The heat transmitted quickly through the air. Before he could blink, there was an intense pressure in the atmosphere. The car shuddered and exploded like a bomb.

Kirra had made it several feet away and began running toward him. He watched her as if everything was in slow motion, saw a piece of metal that had broken from the exploded car flying toward her. It was going to pierce her body and impale her from the back to the front.

Zach darted toward Kirra, grabbed her outstretched arm, and pulled her toward him. He swiveled, knowing someone had to take the hit. He angled his left shoulder and could feel the impact of the metal as it penetrated his flesh.

CHAPTER 7

Leon kicked the man hard, sending him back to the concrete floor. He heard the woman crying, but he couldn't let the man stand up and attack him again. Leon knew now the man was a shapeshifter. But why had he wanted to capture Leon? And why didn't his mother seem to know? He could take this opportunity to kill the shapeshifter. But it didn't seem right to kill a half-conscious man in front of his grieving mother. Leon cursed. He had no idea when he'd grown so sentimental. He tied the man to a chair and left the basement.

Back on the street, Leon looked around and felt the impact of the strange environment on him. He walked away from the theater, found a quiet corner, and opened the map again. He knew it wasn't drawn to scale, but he found the spot that indicated Wagga Wagga. At least he knew he needed to head west.

"You need help?" a man who appeared to be in his sixties asked. He looked at Leon with a warm smile on his face.

People on Earth are so friendly, Leon thought. He nodded and pointed to Wagga Wagga on the map. "I need to go there."

The man looked at the map. "You can take the train there."

Leon frowned. "What sort of training should I take?"

The man stared at him blankly then spoke slowly. "No, you don't need training to go there. What I meant was that you need to go to the train station."

"Oh!" Leon said as he recalled reading something about that in his traveler's guidebook.

The man pointed. "The station is just around the corner. Take the train, and you'll be at Wagga Wagga in a few hours."

Leon thanked the kind man and walked toward the station.

The imposing sign of the train station stared down at Leon. He now understood what a train was. He approached a man who looked as if he was giving instructions and flipped out his map asking for directions. The man gave Leon the number of the correct train platform. Heading in the direction the man had pointed, Leon could see the platform with the correct number. He saw people lining up. He watched as they swiped a card across some kind of a stand, and a waist-high bar lifted to let them through to the platform on the other side where the train waited.

Leon could easily step over the low bar, but he figured it was there for security reasons. If he stepped over the bar without using a card, he would be stopped by the guards. Then he noticed that the bar remained in the air for a short time after a person walked through. That was all the time he needed. He tore out a page of his travel book and folded it to the approximate size of the card he saw people using.

As an elderly woman carrying several bags approached the gate and was busy swiping her card, Leon headed over as if to help her before she dropped her things. She thanked him. He moved his hand quickly across the stand as if swiping a card but in actuality trailed the old woman through the gate before the bar dropped.

He knew he was doing the wrong thing, but the situation called for it. He tucked away his feelings of guilt and walked toward the train.

The train moved at an incredible speed. Although he was transported between the Babylonian court and Earth in the blink of an eye, he had never been able to see the journey or understand how it worked. He couldn't even judge whether it was fast or slow. But from his very comfortable seat looking out the window, he could tell this railway transportation was fast.

"My God!"

Leon jumped out of his skin as he heard the voice of the woman against his ear. But before he could respond, he saw an authoritative-looking man approaching him along the aisle. He was checking people's security cards. It would soon be his turn to show a card he didn't have.

"My God!" the voice said again.

"What do you want?" Leon snarled.

"Please accept my gratitude for not killing my son. I'm not sure what he did to offend you."

"Well, he knocked me out, bit me with his poisonous teeth, and kidnapped me. If I were at the court, I'd send him to the well to fight the two-headed lizards. Let him see whose teeth are sharper."

"I'm sorry—"

"Stop talking. Nobody can see you. And I'm about to be found out by that man over there. I don't have the card he's asking for."

"You mean the ticket? You don't have a ticket for this train?"

"Whatever." Leon grimaced. "I can't exactly jump out of the train right now, can I? It's moving like a storm from an angry god."

"Do you want me to make this problem go away, my God? You only need to say the word."

"What? Can you get me one of those tickets?"

"No, I don't have that kind of power. I can't make things appear out of nothing."

"So what can you do?"

"I can make your problem go away. Do I have your permission? I only want to show my gratitude."

Leon nodded and waved his hand absently. "Do what you have to do. I don't really want to have to jump out of this moving train."

In the blink of an eye, the security man grabbed his chest and fell to the floor of the train.

"He had a heart attack. Do we have a doctor on the train?" somebody yelled out.

"Stop the train!" someone else called out. Some passengers rushed toward the man. More followed. They tried to resuscitate the man.

"I think he's gone," a man said as he checked the man's pulse.

Leon jumped to his feet. He spoke between his teeth. "What did you do? I didn't ask you to kill him!"

"You gave me permission to make the problem go away, my God."

"But I didn't ask you to kill the man. Surely there was another way? Can you take back what you did?"

"I am sorry, my God. The only thing I can do is to take souls away. I can't put them back."

"What are you? Death?"

"No, my God. But I used to be one of his apprentices. I am a soul trader."

CHAPTER 8

Zach grabbed the piece of metal in his shoulder and pulled it out. If Kirra had been stabbed by this while standing by the car explosion, she would have resembled exactly the vision Mya had seen—Kirra dead, floating in fire, a knife piercing her heart. Now that he had taken the stab, he thought he had saved her—at least from this particular lethal incident. But he knew the pain-in-the-neck lynx would soon do something else since she hadn't been able to kill Kirra this time.

A short distance away, the lynx had stood up and changed itself back into a woman's form. She looked as if she was ready for a second attack. Hand-to-hand combat with his daggers would ward her off, but he wasn't sure it would kill the shapeshifter. She seemed to keep coming back. So Zach concentrated and tried his unique talent—his sound waves. He used it mostly to annoy people and had never before used it to kill. But this time, he might have to. He was a sound-bender after all.

He sent a blast of sound at Elanora. Not just any sound. This was the sound he had heard from the old female lynx he and Leon had killed in their hotel room.

Elanora let out a bloodcurdling scream when the sound hit her.

It worked! Zach thought and continued to blast more sound.

The woman staggered back and slumped to the ground on her knees.

Zach kept shooting the waves in her direction. Her skin glowed in a burning red shade as if she were a piece of iron in a furnace. Zach was sure she was going to melt.

He blasted the sound. More. And more.

Suddenly, the woman looked up. Her skin color now looked as if it had started to cool down.

When Zach's sound waves encountered strong resistance, they bounced back at him twice as hard. There was no mistaking it when the sound hit him. The force was so strong it pushed him backward and lifted him off the ground. He landed on his backside. He stood up, cursed, and blasted again.

The sound hit the woman. She roared—and it bounced back at Zach. He fell again but sprung up to his feet and blasted at her again. He wasn't sure how long he could sustain this fight. The woman seemed to cool down quickly, and each blast from him appeared to have less impact on her—and cause more damage to himself.

Then Kirra charged past him with the piece of metal he had just pulled out from his shoulder in her hand. She was fast. So fast he couldn't grab her and hold her back. Kirra said nothing but shoved the jagged metal straight into Elanora's heart.

Elanora let out a dreadful scream.

Kirra pulled the metal out and stabbed again.

The lynx burst into flame, and the force of the sudden heat pushed Kirra backward.

Elanora's eyes sparked with fire. The two women stood, staring at each other. Zach darted toward Kirra, but the heat forced him back like a tidal wave. Elanora let out another chilling scream and then exploded into nothingness.

Kirra stood still. So still it was scary. From behind, Zach couldn't see her face. But he saw her skin turn white and blue and then return to normal skin tone, all within a few seconds.

Zach rushed over. He didn't touch her at first. *She might break like crystal,* he thought. He walked around to the front of her. She was looking down, and he couldn't see her face.

"Kirra!" he said softly.

There was no response.

He touched her chin gingerly, tilting her face up. "Kirra, please don't scare me." Her eyes were as glassy and empty as Mya's in her deity mode. Kirra stared at him blankly as if seeing through him. Then she fell into his arms.

CHAPTER 9

Mya ran as fast as she could with Zach's wrist unit in her hand. She had cleared quite a distance with the leopards. She couldn't believe they could be that slow. They didn't seem to be able to catch up with her at all. Or maybe she was faster than she gave herself credit for. It was suddenly quiet. *Have I completely cut you all loose?* she thought, but she kept running. It could be a trap, something to try to get her to slow down. For a while, only the quietness followed her. *This can't be right.* If she kept running, she might end up back at the Babylonian court. She stopped and turned around. The serenity of the Australian outback stared back at her—the animals were nowhere to be seen.

"Where did you all go?" she asked. But she decided to return to where Zach and Kirra were. In the distance, she could see Zach stepping out from what looked like a war zone with Kirra in his arms.

She darted over. "What happened?" she asked, looking at Kirra. She knew Kirra hadn't died. She didn't sense her death, nor did she see it on Zach's face.

"She killed the lynx," Zach said.

"She killed it? You mean it's dead? Of course it is. Otherwise, you wouldn't have said it was. But how is that possible? A lynx of Elanora's caliber can't be killed by a human. What did she use to kill her?" she asked, not expecting an answer.

"Will she be okay?" Zach asked.

"Oh, I'm sorry. Yes, I think she'll be okay. I didn't sense her death."

Zach let out a sigh of relief. "Let's find a place where she can rest. She stabbed the woman, and the woman burst into flames. Kirra looked as if she were going to break like crystal. Then she passed out. I didn't see her get injured..."

Before Mya could say anything, Kirra stirred in Zach's arms and opened her eyes.

"How are you feeling, Kirra?" Zach asked.

She looked at him groggily, then she turned and looked at Mya. "Let me down," Kirra said.

Zach put her down. She could stand on her own, but he held on to her shoulders to steady her before letting go. "Do you remember what you just did?" he asked.

She looked at him, and then she looked at Mya. She gasped and glanced around. "You took Zach's wrist unit and lured the leopards away!"

"Yes, I did," Mya said. "On that note, here you are, Zach." She gave the unit back to Zach. "I thought I had outrun the animals, but it appears you've killed the lynx, and that's what caused the leopards to disappear."

"I didn't kill it. I shot at it, but it didn't die, and it got really mad."

Zach stared at Mya. She looked at him, and he knew she was wondering why Kirra didn't remember her kill shot. Zach opened his mouth and was about to ask, but Mya cut in. "Kirra, it's like a war zone here. You both must have put up a hell of a fight. And your shoulder is bleeding, Zach." She looked at Zach as she spoke. At the same time, she switched on her deity mode in a flash to peek into Kirra's mind. She knew Zach saw and understood what she was trying to do. He looked at her and said nothing.

In Kirra's mind, Mya saw nothing else except what she had just verbalized.

"Oh yeah, the bleeding is quite bad," Zach muttered and pressed the heel of his hand to the wound.

Kirra scowled. "Don't do that. It'll bleed more."

Mya switched off her deity mode and looked at Zach. She shook her head slightly, signaling that she had found nothing unusual in Kirra's mind.

"Let's find a place for you two to rest, and we'll plan the next step," Mya said as she glanced around. They were in the middle of nowhere. Endless red dirt hills sprawled to the left of them, and a thick forest flanked the country road to the right. Mya didn't think they had a chance of finding an inn nearby.

"There's a small inn a couple miles west," Kirra said.

Mya had totally forgotten Kirra worked as a tour guide. She smiled. "That's headed back in the direction of Wagga Wagga. So we're going backward. But let's stay there for the night," Mya said.

"And we'll need another car. It'll take a lifetime to walk to Sydney," Zach said.

"What about teleporting?" Mya asked.

Zach glanced at Kirra then back at Mya. "Sure, but we'll have to wait until nighttime. I still haven't got a hundred percent hang of the landing end of it. We don't want to suddenly appear in the middle of a shopping mall."

"Or we can take a side trip. Head south a bit and get to the train station for the interstate train line. The express will take us to Sydney in a few hours. That way, we don't need a car," Kirra said.

"That's brilliant." Zach grinned.

Mya hesitated. "Taking the train?"

"What's the problem, Mya?" Kirra asked.

She shook her head. "Nothing. Let's go." She had an odd feeling about this. Something was about to go wrong. But she didn't know what it was.

"If you're sensing something, we need to know now, Mya," Zach said.

"The train is a confined moving box..."

Zach chuckled. "Yes, we all know that, Mya. It's inflexible. We don't have control over it. But if we want to get to Leon quickly—and get back so that we can get back to Eudaiz, get your jar of potion, and pay your debts to the Goddess—that would be the quickest way. We can go to the hotel, and I can teleport tonight, but I really can't wait another nanosecond to get back to Eudaiz."

Kirra frowned. "What's your concern, Mya? What's the problem?" she asked again.

Mya cleared her throat to buy some time, then she looked at Kirra. "All right, I'll lay all the cards on the table. We don't have time to play mind games and, like Zach, I want to get to Leon as soon as possible. He's not equipped to be going around in this world by himself."

Kirra smiled. "Bring it on."

"Zach said you stabbed the lynx to death, and then you passed out. But you don't remember the incident."

Kirra shrugged. "Must be a post-traumatic reaction."

"I wish it was that simple, Kirra. A lynx of Elanora's caliber can't be killed by a human. I don't know exactly what her rank is, but she's no ordinary lynx. I don't even know how to kill her myself, but I do know this. A high-ranking lynx can choose to shift from one bodily host to another."

Zach raised his hand. "Wait, you're not saying Elanora possessed Kirra, are you?"

Kirra's eyebrows raised. "For your information, I feel more like myself than ever before."

Mya shook her head. "I'm not drawing any conclusions...yet."

"All right, what do you need to know or do to be sure?" Kirra asked.

"I have to look into your soul."

"What?" Kirra exclaimed.

Zach raked his hand through his hair. "I know you can switch on your deity mode and search people's lives and even their destiny. But looking into someone's soul is a serious violation of privacy, Mya."

"I know. That's why I rarely do it. And I can only do it with the person's permission."

"Like lie detection exercises in spy movies?" Kirra asked.

Zach laughed. "You have a way of making things light and easy, Kirra. You don't have to agree to do this. But please understand there are a lot of things at stake—"

"I do," Kirra cut in. "I understand. I don't have important things to do in my life like you two do, but I understand that your decisions have an impact on other's lives. So I don't mind a little lie detection. I have nothing to hide." She smiled and looked at Mya. "And if you see any girly secrets in my soul while you're there, please don't tell anyone else about them!"

Mya smiled. "I promise."

"What do I have to do?"

"Nothing. Just close your eyes and relax."

Kirra followed her instructions, and Mya approached. She raised her hands up, hovering them just above Kirra's head but not touching it. Then she closed her eyes, switched on her deity mode, and floated into her subconscious deity division where she could look into people's souls.

There, she saw Kirra's.

CHAPTER 10

Richard left the office after the meeting with the board directors of the theatrical company. After Casey passed away, the estimated loss for the company had been so tremendous that they couldn't continue the show right away. Casey had an understudy, but she was far from ready, so based on Richard's recommendation, they tentatively rescheduled the next performance. He decided to stay with the company for a little longer to sort things out.

Richard had decided not to tell the directors that Casey hadn't died but had vanished into thin air right in front of him. He was sure it was the right decision. He tried to blame what he thought he had seen on a hallucination. It seemed logical since he had blacked out immediately afterward. It surprised him that the doctor and nurse who had seen the incident as well had remained silent about it.

He needed time to mull things over and figure out what was actually going on. He was uncertain about so many things. But there was one thing he knew for sure—this theatrical company wasn't what it appeared to be in the public eye.

He walked past Casey's room on his way out and stopped at the door. It made no difference now whether she had died or just disappeared. The fact remained that she had vanished from his life. The pain hit him like a storm. He hadn't thought about that since leaving the hospital. He'd deliberately avoided thinking about it. Now the feelings of loss were taking a toll on him. He pushed open the door to her room and stepped into the world of Casey Anderson.

The room was the same as he remembered it. It wasn't like he'd had a chance to spend a lot of time here, but he absorbed as much information about her as possible whenever he came here. He could still smell the faint scent of her perfume. So feminine and earthy.

A luxurious bed rested in the middle of the room, grand and inviting. It was so Casey. She always talked about the freedom of the subconscious when the human mind was in a dream state. That was why the bed was central in her life. It wasn't just about sleeping. It was about traveling to a world where her mind could be free of earthly worries.

For her, the velvet and silky linen were an integral part of the sleeping experience. Surprising for a performer, she didn't have a large makeup desk or an endless wardrobe. She didn't need accessories, Richard mused. Her beauty and talent had best represented her in this world. Or maybe in his mind. He traced his finger on the pillow, feeling the softness of the fabric of the pillowcase. He sat down on the bed and picked it up. At the very back of the neat arrangement of pillows and cushions of all sizes on the bed, he saw the corner of a small wooden box.

He pulled the box out and examined it. It was an exquisite antique box, and he was sure whatever was inside must be precious to Casey. It was unlocked. He frowned. Maybe what was inside wasn't as important as he thought. Maybe it was just some herbs and flowers she used to help induce sleep.

But he wasn't going to open the box. That would invade her privacy. Regardless of whether she was dead or alive, he could at least respect her privacy. He stared at the box, and it stared back at him in challenge. Casey had disappeared right in front of him. A man had tried to take her out of the hospital. The man said she would trade a life for Richard. What did he mean by that?

What if he could find an answer in this box? What if it could help him find Casey?

He rubbed his thumb over the copper lock, then he flipped it over and opened the box.

CHAPTER 11

The interstate train pulled into a small station. Leon stood up and bolted toward the door. He had changed to another cabin, but he couldn't get the image of the dead security man out of his mind. It was his first kill under his command on Earth, executed by an apprentice of Death—a soul trader.

He knew of the soul traders. He'd never met one, let alone had one under his command. And this one kept referring to him as God. Leon shook his head, trying to make sense of things.

An announcement was broadcast from a speaker—"Please note that this is an emergency stop because of an incident on board. This is not a station on our normal route. You may choose to depart the train here, but be aware it might cause a disruption in your planned journey. If you stay onboard, we will soon be back on the main route. The next station is Middle Land."

"My God, you shouldn't get off the train because the next train at this station won't get you to where you want to be."

"How do you know where I want to be? And I sent you away. I don't want to hear your voice anymore. Go away."

"As you wish, my God."

"Wait..." Leon said after a moment of hesitation.

"Yes, my God. I am still here."

"Why do you keep calling me God?"

"You have the light of God around you. The sort of light that only a soul trader like me can see. We were taught that your soul cannot be traded. You are one of the gods. What kind of god, I do not know."

"Right. So am I immortal? I can't be killed?"

"No, my God. Your soul might be immortal. But your body may not be. You might be able to travel from life to life through incarnation. That's my speculation. All I know is that I cannot take your soul and trade it as I did with the human earlier."

Leon nodded. "So who are you, and why did your son kidnap me?"

Silence.

Leo continued. "By taking that long to answer, I assume you're coming up with some kind of lie. So don't worry about it."

"Please forgive me, my God."

"There's nothing for me to forgive. Tell your son to leave me alone."

"Yes, my God."

"What's your name? That has to be something you don't have to lie about."

"Currently, I am called Casey Anderson."

"Currently? So you change your name often? Are you a fugitive?"

"I have a situation that I don't care to talk about. It has caused me to float around for more than a thousand years in different human forms. During each human life, I have a different identity. But in a sense, yes, I am a fugitive. My son believes there's a way out of this..." She sobbed. "He believes he can save me... He's a good boy... But I don't know why he tried to capture you. I haven't had a chance to talk to him yet."

"What are you hiding or escaping from? Your son tried to save you and kidnapped me. So there must be a connection between the two.

There must be something I can do to help your situation. Why did you have to float around for a thousand years?

"My God, do you really want to help me?"

"Only if it doesn't involve anything morally wrong. What do you need?"

"I don't know what's right and wrong, my God. I was born and raised as a soul trader, and that is all I do. I receive orders, I take souls, and I trade them."

"Who gives you the orders?"

"My God!"

"If you want my help, you have to tell me the truth."

Silence.

"Casey!"

The only thing Leon could hear now was the murmuring the of passengers in the other cabin. He was the only one in his cabin, and it was dead quiet. Casey had gone. He felt a bit uneasy. At least the invisible soul trader spoke Babylonian and appeared to be on his side. But now he was back to being alone in this strange world.

The train started to move toward the next station. They'd announced the next destination, but he hadn't paid attention. His mind wandered back to the moment the black cat got him when he was in the basement, and then the encounter with Casey and the cat again in a man's form.

As Leon went backward in his mind and traced every step to see if he could draw any conclusions, the train headed toward Middle Land.

CHAPTER 12

Mya opened her eyes. She could feel Zach's breath right against her neck as he stood behind her. She turned around, and Zach's face was so close he could almost kiss her. But there was no romance in his eyes. He was waiting for her response regarding Kirra. Mya knew that was one of Zach's problems—he cared too much for those he considered his friends.

She smiled. Her smile seemed to lift the weight of worry from Zach's shoulders. "So it's all good?" he asked.

She nodded.

"Can you wake her now?" Zach asked.

Kirra was still standing, her eyes closed as if hypnotized. "Before I bring her back, I have to tell you this, Zach. Although I can't see anything unusual about her soul right now, it doesn't mean she won't change. Magical lynxes cannot be killed by ordinary humans. That's a fact. The way you described the incident, I think she looked into Elanora's eyes before she killed her. That was the perfect chance for the lynx to jump into a new host body."

Zach raked his hands through his hair. "So what are we supposed to do? How can we tell?"

"There's not much we can do now. I just want you to be careful. Also, it's the same deal you have with Leon. You told Leon he's carrying the eudqi of Eudaiz, and if he's captured by Eudaiz's adversaries, you'll have to kill him before the eudqi is taken. It's the same with Kirra."

"How so?"

"If Elanora did happen to take over Kirra's soul, I will have to kill her. And trust me, Zach, I would be doing her a favor. There's nothing worse than being possessed by a devil soul."

"You said a lynx can't be killed."

"It can't be killed by an ordinary human. Or even a minor god. I can't kill it. But a soul is different. I can't kill a soul, but I can destroy it by locking it in the underworld."

"Like putting it in jail?" Zach raised an eyebrow.

Mya nodded. "Yes, like that. I have the authority to do that. But it requires the destruction of the physical body."

Zach shook his head. "So it's similar to a kill. But you said you can't physically kill a lynx!"

Mya sighed. "It's complicated, isn't it? Not all lynx are bad. If they don't do anything wrong, I can't kill them. But possessing someone else's soul is wrong, and on those grounds, my power can kill it."

Zach scowled. "So if that's the case, Kirra is a sacrificial lamb. She didn't do anything wrong but will be killed because an evil lynx possessed her soul."

Mya nodded. "Unfortunately, yes. I don't want it to go down that way. Just like you don't want to have to kill Leon. But as you can see, it's a little complicated."

Zach nodded. "All right. We'll see how it goes." He approached her. "I know what the whole eudqi ordeal costs me. But what will this cost you? If you send an evil soul to the underworld, it's going to cost you something. It can't be as easy as it sounds."

"The only thing is that I am only a minor deity. I don't have a lot of power. If I run into a strong magical creature, I'll have to put up a fight. And I don't always win those sorts of fights."

Zach tilted her chin up. "Just like marrying a cop..."

"Is that a proposal?"

"I thought I already proposed, and you already said yes."

"No, I didn't—"

He cut off her speech with a bone-melting kiss. They held each other for a while before Mya turned to wake Kirra.

Kirra opened her eyes. "That seemed like a very long lie detection session. Did I pass?" she asked.

Zach grinned. "It seems you did. Shall we go to the train station, Ms. Tour Guide?"

Kirra shrugged. "See, I told you. As a part of my training, I'm very resilient. I almost joined the army."

"Really? I didn't know that." Zach laughed and wrapped his arm around her shoulders. He looked back and winked at Mya. Mya smiled and followed Zach and Kirra. She still felt uneasy, but she had no proof of her suspicion and no way to explain the butterflies she had in her stomach right now.

In no time, they were settled in their seats on a train to Sydney. An announcement let them know that the next station would be Middle Land.

CHAPTER 13

Richard startled so badly he dropped the wooden box. As soon as he'd opened the box he knew he shouldn't, he'd heard Casey calling his name. He whirled around. A perfume bottle, a necklace charm, and a bracelet scattered on the carpeted floor, having spilled out of the opened box. He gathered them and put them back into the box. He must have imagined Casey's voice.

"Richard," she gently called again.

"Holy sweet Jesus Christ!" he exclaimed. He put the box on the dressing table and scanned the room. "I don't expect to see you because you vanished right in front of me, Casey. But I can hear you now. Does that mean you aren't dead?"

"Richard."

"Yes, you've called me three times, and I heard you each time. Can you tell me what's going on?"

"You're not supposed to open that box, Richard."

"I know. I'm sorry. I put your perfume and the jewelry back inside. If you can't tell me what's going on, that's fine. I understand. But can I see you one more time? Is there a way I can see your face? One more time, Casey?"

"It's not supposed to happen like this, Richard. We're not supposed to have any kind of relationship."

"What do you mean by that? We can't have a relationship? My wife passed away a long time ago. And you're single...unless—"

"No, it's not that."

"So what is it? I know I should have revealed my feelings to you earlier. Do you know what it feels like waking up and being told you might go away forever? And when I finally got to see you on that hospital bed, I watched you fade away right in front of my eyes, and there was nothing I could do about it."

"You're not supposed to have any feelings for me, Richard."

"The hell I'm not. And who was the man in the hospital room? Why did he say you traded a life for me? I swear I saw a falling rail backstage, and I pushed you out of the way. If someone was supposed to be dead, that person should be me."

"No, Richard. That rail was for me. I was supposed to die. But I couldn't let you die for me, so I traded a life for yours."

Richard paced back and forth in the room, waving his arms in the air. "I don't know what that means, and I'm not sure I want to. You're supposed to die? For whom? Or for what? And who was the man in your hospital room? He's too young to be your husband."

"He's my son."

Richard stopped pacing. He composed himself and then nodded. "I thought he might be. He looks the same age as my Samantha."

Silence.

"Maybe a little older. He can't be older than his thirties. Otherwise you must have had him when you were ten..."

Silence.

"Casey, are you still here?"

"Yes, Richard."

"Oh, you were a bit quiet. I thought you'd gone. Let's not talk about irrelevant matters. Now that you're around, there must be a way you can get back here and be normal."

"I can never be normal, Richard."

"I know there's something magical or supernatural about this. I'm very open-minded. More than you would believe. So if you'll just tell me what's going on and what can I do to fix it, I will."

"I don't want you to be tangled up in this mess."

"I already am! Maybe you can untangle me by telling me the truth."

"You're not ready for this."

"Try me."

CHAPTER 14

Leon leaned up against the window of the train. He was sure the magnificent scenery he was seeing was trivial to many humans living here, but for him, it was a once in a lifetime experience. Endless hillsides and forests flanked the road. The train crossed a hanging bridge over a river, and he had to hold his breath as he looked down. The speed of the train was incredible. He loved everything about this place. But as Zach had told him, Eudaiz was a million times better. He looked forward to going there.

The Babylonian court was beautiful. He lived close to the temple where he worked. He adored the golden architecture, the luxury, and the beautiful clothing people wore to attend court. But there were two things the court had never had. One was a feel of vibrancy and liveliness. People there were alive, of course, but it seemed as if they were alive only because they had to be. And the second thing was Mya. The liveliness. The energy. And the beauty of her.

Now, he had found a third thing the court would never have—Kirra. The lingering sensation and feelings Leon had whenever he was around her were addictive. He didn't know if Zach could take Kirra to Eudaiz, but he knew he would really miss having her around. Hearing her voice, lilting in his ear like a song.

A chill ran down his spine as he heard a low growl. It was more like a hum of evil, echoing somewhere from the middle of the Earth. He didn't know where he got that idea from. It was just there inside his mind, and he didn't care for it.

The door connected to the neighboring cabin slid open, and he saw Casey's son walk in. Leon sprang to his feet. He could kick the guy's backside and turn him into a puddle of mud right now, but there were innocent people in the cabin, and Leon didn't want collateral damage to stain the experience of his trip.

The man came over and sat down opposite Leon.

"I don't want innocents to die if we fight in here. Your mother isn't around. Nobody will beg for you."

"I tied you up and held you in a basement before. Why do you think it would be any different this time?"

"Two reasons. I didn't kill you when I had the chance. Even shapeshifters have a code of honor. You ought to pay me back. Second, you took me off guard because I didn't think a big leopard like you would bite like a kitten. Now that I know, I won't let you bite me. If we go one on one on level ground, I'll kick your ass."

The man chuckled. "One way to find out. The next station is Middle Land. We can go out for a run."

"I'm sure we can do more than just running." Leon sized up the man. He was tall, strong, and might be a skilled fighter. He hadn't had a real fight with this man, but he was sure he wouldn't beat him easily at his one hundred percent capacity. He'd love a chance to test his combat skill in this world. But he did remember he was here because of Mya. Until he sorted out that mission, he couldn't go around picking fights.

"What's your name?" Leon asked.

The man leaned back in his seat and looked at Leon with deep purple eyes. "Dex."

"Why do you want to capture me, Dex? What do you want from me? If it's about your mother, what do you want me to do for her?"

"Why do you want to help my mother?"

"She seemed like a good person apart from that fact that she killed the ticket man. But I guess that's her job."

"Don't think you know everything just from a little conversation with her," Dex growled.

"All right. I don't know everything. So entertain me. What exactly do you want from me?"

"I want your blood."

Leon chuckled. "Well, I don't mind donating some blood if it'll be of help."

Dex shrugged. "Not *some* blood. I need *all* of your blood."

Leon smiled. "I'm afraid I'm not that generous. And for your information, your mother called me a god, and she, although a soul trader, can't trade my soul. That's what she said."

Dex arched an eyebrow. "You exchanged quite a bit of information in a little conversation with my mother."

"Does the fact that she called me God change anything? Do you think my blood can still help her?"

"Are you afraid to fight me?"

Leon shook his head. "If we don't fight, I can save your mother the heartache of your death, Dex."

"You're overconfident."

"I'm just stating a fact. I am the head of the temple guards at the Babylonian court. I've been in combat for hundreds of years. What can you do except use your poisonous teeth behind people's backs?"

The train slowly approached the station and stopped. As soon as the door slid open, Leon grabbed Dex and threw him outside, rolling out with him onto the train platform. Before the people there had time to react, Dex and Leon had run off the platform and darted down the hill.

CHAPTER 15

Mya leaned into Zach's chest and snuggled comfortably in his arms. They were sitting in a cabin toward the back of the train heading toward Sydney. Kirra was right—this was a smooth means of transportation. The best thing about it was that she got to sit next to Zach, and he didn't have to drive. She liked the feel of his warm body. She liked hearing his breathing and his heartbeat. The gash on his left shoulder from the stab wound he had taken for Kirra had almost healed. He had told her if it happened in Eudaiz, he could go to his chamber, and the healing process would be instant. But it was healing now, so that was good enough.

She couldn't wait to finish this mission. She wanted to find Leon and get the jar of potion back to Ishtar to pay off her debts. Then she could travel with Zach and Leon to Eudaiz, a universe she was sure had been designed for true happiness. She would never again have to count the balance of lives she saved and killed. She could get a job that had nothing at all to do with numbers.

"That's Leon!" Kirra exclaimed from the seat behind them and pointed toward a stretch of woods a short distance away. Zach and Mya looked out the window and could see Leon and another man running and then fighting each other among the trees. It was quite a distance away, and most people wouldn't recognize the shapes of the two men fighting. But for Mya, it was unmistakably Leon, his athletic body hopping up and down along the tree line.

She felt deliriously happy. He was alive and obviously doing quite well.

The train eased into the Middle Land train station. As soon as the cabin door slid open, the trio charged out to the platform and zoomed down the hillside.

When they closed the distance, Mya called out, "Leon!"

When Leon turned and saw the trio, he grinned. At the same time, the man who was fighting with him scowled. *You'd better scowl,* Mya thought with a smile. *We're here, and you're a dead man.* Four against one wasn't exactly fair, but when they'd fought packs of leopards, a fair fight hadn't seemed to be on the leopards' list of game rules.

But before the grin could fade from Mya's face, silhouettes of animal shapes appeared in the woods opposite them. They growled.

The man fighting with Leon took a step backward with a smirk on his face. He raised a hand and signaled. The leopards charged forward, and they would get to Leon first.

"Damn it!" Mya cursed and ran toward Leon.

"Don't, Mya. There are too many of them. You can't help!" Zach shouted.

She heard Zach curse behind her, but she couldn't wait for him and Kirra. She had to give Leon a hand. She switched her deity mode on and ran like the wind across the open field of wildflowers and small shrubs, heading toward the thick woods.

She could see the edge of the woods. The animals moved closer, still at the far end. Leon had been quick enough to grab the man before he could get away. He landed punches and kicks on him without mercy. The man appeared to be physically bigger and stronger than Leon, but with Leon's hundreds of years serving the court as the head of the temple guard and being a good warrior himself, the man didn't stand a chance.

Leon could see the animals approaching him. Mya had no idea how he would be able to fight them all. Even if she was with him, it wouldn't help. She understood now why Zach was cursing and why he kept saying she was impulsive. But the situation called for it, didn't it? Maybe not. Perhaps she would be better off figuring out a way for herself and Leon to escape the storm of fur and claws heading their way.

"Leave him! Run, Leon!" She waved her hands frantically, gesturing for him to run toward her.

He ignored her and stomped more kicks on the man on the ground. It was unlike Leon, but he appeared to be royally pissed off with the guy.

"Come on, Leon. The leopards are coming. There are too many of them."

Leon looked up and saw the animals approaching. He froze with his leg in the air mid-kick. That was when he realized it wasn't just him facing the wave of animals—Mya was right there with him. He cursed. He grabbed the man on the ground and pulled him up, pressing the blade of the knife against his throat. Mya knew Leon was trying to make the man command the animals to withdraw. *Smart move*, she thought.

The man turned his head, and Leon immediately released him as if afraid. The man shifted into a gigantic black cat, roared, and leaped away. Leon stood, staring. On the one hand, there was a sea of animals approaching. On the other hand, Mya was there, ready to support him.

"Come here, Leon!" Mya called out again, but she knew Leon wouldn't run toward her now. He could see the situation. She could run away fast. He couldn't. And if he ran toward her, she would wait for him, and the animals would chase him. They would end up being a meat feast for the pack. But there was no way she was going to leave him.

Leon looked at her. Then he turned around and ran away from her.

"Leon!" she shouted again.

But he ignored her and kept running. The animals paused a second, seeming confused by Leon's change in direction. Some of them turned immediately to chase him. But others stood, eyeing Mya. "Come on, who do you want? Leon or me?" Mya muttered.

CHAPTER 16

Zach pressed a series of buttons on his wrist unit. He wished he had paid more attention when Ciaran had tried to give him instructions on how to use it properly. It was too late now, so this had to work. He had to take care of the leopards using some means other than direct fighting. There were too many of them.

Zach looked up and could see Leon had run away from Mya. The ocean of furry animals was confused and stuck in the middle. His wrist unit wasn't responding the way he wanted.

"Why don't you use voice command?" Kirra asked.

"This is more accurate," he lied. By using voice command, he would be giving out a lot of information including his passcode, his trigger pin, and some secret keywords that only he and his keyboard knew. Zach didn't know who was listening. He tried to refrain from even thinking about the information just in case a mind reader tried to peek in.

He shook his head and entered more commands, cursing when the machine denied him. He looked up and saw that the group of animals had split in half. One half of them chased Leon, and the other half headed toward Mya.

Zach continued working on the wrist unit. It was the only solution he could think of at the moment. They heard a low growl from behind them. Without looking back, Zach cursed. "Oh, for fuck's sake. If you want to bite me, come out. There's no need to growl." He turned around, and a furry black cat that looked like the one that had attacked him before came out of the bush.

The cat slunk back and forth, figuring out the best way to attack. Kirra pulled out her knife. "I'll take care of it, Zach. You figure out your machine before the leopards eat Leon and Mya alive."

"I can't let you do that. It's an enormous cat."

"Watch me!" Kira said as she slowly approached the cat.

"Don't be ridiculous, Kirra."

"Shhh, it's watching me. See, it's not attacking. So calm down. Let me do the talking." She looked at the cat. "Let me handle this. It doesn't look aggressive."

Zach stepped back and worked frantically on his wrist unit.

The cat and Kirra approached each other slowly. "Hey. Meow. Nice and gentle. Come here. What do you want, black cat? Do I know you? You look like the one I saw in the bush before."

The cat actually looked less aggressive as Kirra got closer.

"What is that? Are you hypnotizing it?" Zach asked.

"Whatever it is I'm doing, it's working. Now you focus on your job, or you'll lose your two friends over there."

Zach muttered some profanity as the machine kept foiling him. He glanced over at Kirra and saw her raise her hand up and then lower it.

In front of his astonished eyes, the cat sat.

"Good boy," Kirra said. "I'm guessing you're a boy, in which case you wouldn't like being patted on the head. So what are you looking for here?"

Zach's wrist unit beeped a happy sound. "I got it!" he shouted. He raised his arm, signaling to Mya, and spoke as he ran. "Leave the cat, Kirra."

He ran a few more steps, but sensing Kirra wasn't following, he stopped. "Kirra, leave the cat. Follow me."

"It's sitting. It might leap if I turn my back on it," she said between her teeth.

"I can't leave you here staring at the cat. Can you put it to sleep or something, given it's hypnotized?"

"I don't know how to put it to sleep. I didn't hypnotize it."

"So why is it staring at you?"

"I don't know. I don't even know if it's staring at me or looking straight ahead. It's obviously not speaking to me."

Zach approached and gently pulled Kirra's arm. "Step aside slowly."

She did. The cat kept staring ahead.

"All right. So it's not staring at you. It's somehow frozen," Zach muttered. "And you're right, turning our backs to it might be a bad idea."

"Sleep!" Kirra said.

The cat didn't move.

"Nice try, Kirra... All right, I think I have to do this," Zach said and pulled his knife out.

"It's not attacking you, Zach."

"It might if we turn around and it comes out of its coma or daydream or whatever status it's in at the moment."

"Please don't kill the cat." Kirra had tears in her eyes.

"We need to get to the other two now. If it leaps at us, we'll be meat." Zach pressed his dagger against the cat's neck. It didn't move, didn't duck, didn't even growl. He looked into its eyes. He thought they were green at first, but he could see a shade of purple in them now.

It was strange—he just couldn't make himself slide the dagger to slit the cat's throat. He'd killed many cats on the way here. This was just another one. But it was like an defenseless man, and he couldn't bring himself to kill it.

"Stay. If you follow us, I'll cut your throat for real." The enormous cat looked at him. It was so close to him he could hear its breathing. It looked as though it had tears in its eyes.

"I mean it. Don't think you can shed your cat's tears and I won't kill you. I think you're the one that attacked me before. And I haven't gotten even with you. So don't you move an inch."

Zach eased the knife away from the cat's neck. He locked his eyes on it for a while to be sure it wasn't moving. The he turned to Kirra. "Let's go. If it leaps, I'll finish it off."

"Are you sure, Zach? I'll let go. I'll stop looking at it now."

"Okay, ease off slowly. Take it slow. There you go," Zach said as Kirra turned around. He took a last look to make sure the cat remained still. Then they charged in Mya and Leon's direction.

"Do you have a plan, Zach?" Kirra asked while running.

"Sort of."

"What do you mean?"

"I have a plan...in theory. But I don't know if it'll work."

"Go away you two!" Mya shouted from a distance.

"Is she yelling at us?" Zach asked.

"I think so!" Kirra grinned and ran faster.

"Are you crazy? Go away!" Leon shouted.

"He really wants us to come rescue him, Zach." Kirra giggled as she spoke.

Zach could see she liked Leon. Now he could see how great a person she was. He had never paid enough attention to her. Not attention in a sexual way, but more like she was a little sister.

Kirra was a few years older than his sister, but he would love her just as much. Leon was a lucky guy, he thought. Kirra was beautiful and gracious, and she was a good person. "Leon certainly needs help. Let's do it!" Zach chuckled and kept running.

They got close enough and stood right between Mya and Leon.

Zach focused. He looked at the running animals and pressed a button on his wrist unit.

CHAPTER 17

Mya understood Zach's intention now. He stood still as the leopards came closer. Then he did something on his wrist unit. Transparent circles of thin air appeared in front of the leopards. The air within the circles wavered like steam evaporating from a hot surface. The leopards jumped through the circles and disappeared.

It was just like in a circus show when animals jump through gigantic hoops of fire. Except there was no fire around these gigantic circles, and the leopards didn't come out the other side. Mya knew Zach had opened a dimensional gateway, and the animals were stupid enough to keep jumping into the circles, not questioning where the animal just in front of them had gone. Their stupidity was to their advantage. But she couldn't help wondering where the other end of the circles led.

Leon and Kirra rushed toward each other. Kirra looked Leon up and down. "Are you okay?" she asked.

"Yes. And you?" he asked.

"Yes. God, I was worried when the black cat got you." Kirra fussed over him. "That cat was enormous. And you didn't exactly fight it," Kirra said.

Leon scowled. "It bit me when I was off guard. It wasn't a fair fight."

Kirra giggled. "I didn't say it was fair. Just that you killed the other shapeshifters, but for some reason, that cat was able to paralyze you with a single bite."

"It had pointy teeth," Leon said.

"All cats have pointy teeth," Mya said.

"Not the one up the hill. It didn't bite us," Kirra said. "I think it's still sitting there."

"What?" Mya asked.

Zach said, "There was a black cat. It looked like the one that bit Leon, but they all look the same. It came out and just stared at us. Then it sat there. It didn't even move when I was about to kill it."

"Did you kill it?" Leon asked.

"No, it didn't attack. I had no reason to kill it."

They looked again at the leopards around them, all of them focusing on the circles. The animals were attracted to the circles like moths flying into flames.

"Where are you sending them to, Zach?" Mya asked.

"I have no clue. I opened the gateway from this end. I'm not sure where they're going."

"What if they come out in the middle of a crowded city?" Kirra asked.

Zach shook his head. "It won't be in a city on Earth. I chose one of the options that connects the gateway elsewhere. I can't tell where because it was a bunch of ridiculous mumbo-jumbo codes. I only had enough time to locate it away from Earth."

"And it won't be Eudaiz, either, I guess," Mya said and smiled at Zach.

He shook his head. "No, I certainly wouldn't send them to Eudaiz. I just input the destination as the original desired point of origins. The system would triangulate..." Zach trailed off as the last leopard jumped through the hoop and vanished.

Mya looked at Zach, arching an eyebrow. "Triangulate with what?"

"Holy cow!" Zach muttered.

"You triangulate leopards with cows?" Leon asked.

Zach looked at Mya then back at Leon. "I sent them to the point of origin of their attraction. In principle, it would be where you both came from."

"You sent them to the *court*?" Mya gasped.

Leon frowned then said, "It'd be okay if they ended up in the jungle outside the court. Do you know where exactly they're sent?"

Zach shook his head.

Both Mya and Leon suddenly grabbed their ears as they heard a loud gong from the court. When they looked up, an image of Ishtar hovered in the air.

It was unprecedented for Ishtar to communicate directly with people outside the court in this way. It was even stranger for her not to be wearing her usual court outfit with tons of golden beads dangling everywhere and twenty pounds of makeup on her face. Mya looked at her Goddess. Without the makeup and the formal court outfits, Ishtar actually looked quite normal. She looked like a kind woman.

"Why did you send these animals to the court, Mya?" Ishtar asked.

"It wasn't her. It was me. I sent them there by accident," Zach said.

"You don't want Mya's debts to mount up, do you, Zach Flynn? You'd say anything to stop that from happening." Ishtar smiled.

"If you don't want to add these animals to your jungle, I can bring them back here," Zach continued, "but why does sending the cats there add to Mya's debts?"

"There's no need for you to take them back. I've already killed almost all of them. As for the rest, I put them to good use. They'll be used in the Death Well to eat criminals. But before I was able to collect the animals, they got to a village. More than five hundred people perished. That will be added to Mya's record."

"No, that's ridiculous. It was my fault. There has to be another way," Zach snarled.

"I like you, Zach. You make Mya happy. I can see it on her face. She's like my daughter..."

Zach snorted.

Ishtar glared at him and continued, "If you want to pay off Mya's debts, get me the jar of potion right now. Bring it to the court, and I will honor our agreement."

"How long do we have?" Mya asked.

Ishtar smiled graciously. "Until I finish my tea. Now."

"That's impossible, my Goddess," Leon exclaimed.

"Nothing is impossible for a Eudaizian Sciphil. Am I right, Zach?"

Zach nodded. "You'll have it. If I have the jar delivered to the court right now, you will free Mya of all of her debts and duties. Is it a deal?"

"Yes, you have my word."

"Your word isn't enough. I want it in writing."

Ishtar chuckled. "As you request." She raised her hand, and a golden scroll dropped to the ground in front of them. Ishtar's image vanished.

Zach picked up the scroll. "Shit...it's gibberish." He gave the scroll to Mya.

Mya took a look. It was in Babylonian. She read the contract and made sure to check all the fine print.

"Is that what she just promised, Mya?" Zach asked.

Mya nodded.

"So how are you going to get the jar delivered now, Zach?" Kirra asked.

"I need some space to be by myself," Zach said.

Mya knew he was going to call Eudaiz and didn't want anyone around when he did so. She signaled Kirra and Leon to walk away.

CHAPTER 18

Ciaran strode into the control chamber in his tower. It was the last unit of the night in Eudaiz, a universe that a few months ago, Earth time, he didn't even know existed. He was now king of this strange universe—a place that guaranteed true happiness to its citizens.

He shook his head in disbelief. What was the definition of true happiness anyway? How could his ancestors buy into such a naive notion? So much that they made the promise, and then generations down the road, he was yanked out of his comfortable life in London, where he managed his global pharmaceutical conglomerate with ease, and flung into a multiversal war to protect those he had never met.

He slammed his left palm onto the control panel and expected the screen to come up instantly. Perhaps it did, but he slammed his palm again anyway.

"Ciaran LeBlanc, Sciphil Three. King of Eudaiz. Information verified. Access confirmed," a robotic voice said.

"Engage communication channel to Sciphil Four's residence."

"Affirmative."

"Cancel that!" Ciaran said quickly.

The machine hummed briefly and said, "Affirmative."

Ciaran strode back and forth in his chamber. He looked at his hands and found they shook a bit, so he shoved them into his pants pockets. He had been king for only a few days, Eudaizian time. The battle cries still echoed in his head, and the feel of warm blood was still raw in his mind— his blood, the blood of those he loved, and blood from his enemies.

Admittedly, on the scale of all things, the fact that his wife had taken their infant twins to her best friend Sciphil Four's residence should be a trivial matter. But it wasn't. His family meant everything to him. Why didn't Madeline understand that? He had always thought she understood him more than he understood himself.

He flicked the communication channel on again. "Engage communication to Sciphil Four's residence."

"Affirmative."

He switched the channel off immediately and cursed. He couldn't give in to this. He had to stand his ground. He paced back and forth again. A communication signal flashed on the screen. He engaged immediately. "Madeline!"

"Ciaran." It was Zach's voice.

Ciaran cleared his throat. "Yes, Zach."

Zach's image appeared on the screen. "We need the jar of potion now, Ciaran."

Ciaran nodded. "Sure." He strode toward a cabinet and entered the code to open it. He took the jar out.

"How are Madeline and the kids?"

"Fine," Ciaran mumbled. "How do you plan to take this potion to Mya's Goddess? You don't intend to make me holocast it to the Babylonian court, do you? You said you'd come back here for it."

Zach nodded. "Yes, but we ran into a bit of trouble. So could you do me a favor and holocast it for me?"

Ciaran raised an eyebrow. Zach's request was strange, but the situation he was in was also unprecedented. Ciaran considered it too early to draw a conclusion. "You understand the holocast technology, right?"

Zach nodded again. "Yes, I know you have to transport physical objects personally, but for your safety, please do not present yourself. Just drop the jar in the court and go." Zach's image flickered.

Ciaran narrowed his eyes. "I won't do it until you give me a full report of your situation."

Zach's image flickered more rapidly, and he appeared to be yanked out of the screen. Ciaran reached for the control panel. He cursed as he entered endless commands, but Zach's screen remained blank.

Ciaran rushed toward the main screen, turned on another control panel, and engaged. "Jake," he called to his head of central intelligence.

The image of a young man came on. "Yes, Ciaran."

"Use the central databank and locate Sciphil Two, Zach Flynn, for me please."

Jake lowered his voice. "Do you mean using the...*that* databank?"

"Yes." Ciaran stared straight into the screen so Jake could see his determination. He was asking his head of central intelligence to access the EYE databank, the most restricted and powerful databank in the multiverse. It was effectively illegal.

But he and Jake had been working on a way to gain access to small amounts of data without alerting the central robot. And that was the quickest way for Ciaran to locate Zach. Zach was on a personal mission, so his journey log wasn't recorded in the Eudaizian system. The EYE belonged to the Daimon Gate, and being independent of any universe, the EYE could see anything anywhere in the multiverse.

Jake came back quickly onto the screen, and Ciaran switched the communication channel to private mode.

"The location is labeled as Babylonian court. But I'm unsure what it means. It's not a proper dimension. It lines up with Earth in two space dimensions, in a different time dimension. It doesn't make any sense. I don't have a precise location, Ciaran."

"I do. Thank you," Ciaran said and was about to switch off the communication.

"No, you don't know, sir."

Ciaran narrowed his eyes. "What did you just say?"

"I said you don't know the precise location of Sciphil Two, sir. With this information, and if you want to holocast, it's dangerous if the destination is unknown. Getting lost there is worse than going into the oblivion. If you go there by yourself, you might get stuck between dimensions—"

"I said I know. That will be all for now, Jake."

"No, sir. You need your first councillor. You need Madeline and her psychic ability. I know you had some kind of disagreement with her, and she took the children—"

"Jake!" Ciaran snapped. "Do you have a spy device in our bedchamber?"

"No, sir. Just along the corridor outside it. It's a standard security—"

"Okay. I'll sort this out with you later. This intelligence practice of yours invades our privacy too much. I don't like it. I *am* going." Ciaran slammed the control panel off, but Jake's voice echoed back.

"I'll send commanders after you, sir..."

Ciaran shook his head and took a moment to contemplate in the tranquility of his control chamber. The Babylonian court was the trickiest dimension to deal with. Not because of its strange location in time and space but because of its ontological and metaphysical properties.

Ciaran knew no one cared for this explanation, so he didn't explain it to many. He didn't know much about this particular dimension, but there were two things he was sure of. One, it had a lot to do with his weakness— magic. And two, Zach was in deep trouble.

Magic! Ciaran shook his head, making a mental note to himself that he had to be very careful with this. Then he turned on his communication channel and switched to private mode. No system in the multiverse needed to know this. Zach was on a private mission, and Ciaran knew exactly where the Babylonian court was.

He navigated the scan to prepare for a holocast. As Zach had said, he only needed to holocast—the technology that they used to transport holographic images across dimensions—but he cranked it up a notch to teleport the jar to the court. He could leave the jar for Zach and then leave the court. If he didn't step out of the holocast, he wouldn't be in any danger.

A blue needle fanned on the monitor suggesting the scanning was in progress. Then it stopped. Ciaran frowned. It had finished too fast. And the image coming across the screen made his blood run cold. Zach was being dragged out in the middle of a place that looked like a medieval execution ground. His leather jacket was tattered, and there was blood smeared across his face.

The image wasn't clear, and the computer couldn't verify whether the information was authentic. Jake was right—the location was elusive, and Ciaran didn't really know it as well as he thought. He needed more than logical deduction and scientific data. He needed Madeline. Only his wife—his first councillor—with her psychic ability could tell.

It was too late. Ciaran had no choice but to do the holocast right now. He grabbed the control panel and was about to call Jake. But even though Jake was the head of intelligence, he still relied on the system to get work done. As king for only a few days, Ciaran knew he had more enemies than friends in the system. He couldn't afford a mistake.

He grabbed a portable device and shot a message to their bedchamber using a private channel to which only he and Madeline had access. She would get the message and know where he had gone. If she came back, that was.

Ciaran returned to the control panel, grabbed the jar of potion, tucked daggers and guns inside his vest, and holocasted off Eudaiz.

In front of him was a haze of dust. Steam from the heat rose up from the ground. In the distance, he could see soldiers about to execute Zach. They dragged him up a raised platform and threw his body onto the floor.

Nobody seemed to see Ciaran. He moved his holocast light beam a bit closer to the execution platform. He couldn't see clearly, but he was afraid that wasting even a second might cost Zach his life. Ciaran pulled his guns out. He was a two-hand shooter. But with what seemed to be a small army out there, he had to be quick. He moved the light beam closer. To shoot at them, he'd have to step out of the protective holocast and be present.

He drew in a breath and charged outside. He ran straight to the execution platform. With a gun in each hand, he dropped all the soldiers on his way with ease. The small army was taken off guard, and they backed out, confused.

Ciaran jumped on the platform. "Zach!" he called. But Zach didn't move. He tucked a gun away, still holding one, and reached down to Zach's shoulder. As soon as he flipped Zach's body over, he knew something was wrong.

Ciaran jerked his left shoulder back. His fatal eudqi point was located at the front of his left shoulder, and before he had any chance to figure out what to do about this fatal weakness and do something to protect all of his councillors, he would have to do his best to avoid getting hit at that point.

The man in Zach's form leaped to his feet, shifted into a soldier, and ran for Ciaran. Ciaran didn't even blink. He pointed his gun and pulled the trigger. The man's head exploded.

But as soon as his body flopped to the floor, the head grew back, and he stood back up. It was the same with the other soldiers Ciaran had killed. They all stood up, and they all had the same mummy look in their eyes.

Just then, Ciaran heard a clapping sound.

A golden round platform appeared, hovering in the air. On it stood a man with skin that looked like it had been dusted in gold. He looked like a statue of a pharaoh straight out of a pyramid. "That was quite a stunt, Ciaran LeBlanc," he said. "You've lived up to your reputation in the multiverse, given the short time you've held a position of power."

"Let me guess—you're not in a position of power. Because if you were, you wouldn't have to use a stunt to get me to your place." Ciaran gestured widely. "Or whatever it is you call this filthy place."

The man laughed. "You're right. I don't have any power. But if I fulfill the contract I have on your head, I'll be able to afford a much better place. But I'm afraid I won't be able to send you an invitation at that point. I don't invite dead people to my house."

CHAPTER 19

Mya's palms were sweaty, and her teeth were clenched. She was nervous like she had never been before. Streaks of cold sweat ran down her spine irrespective of the stinking hot weather of the Australian outback. "Let Zach go. I'll get you what you want."

Kirra stood behind Zach. Her eyes were blank. Her skin cracked, and claws poked out from her fingertips. She grabbed Zach's shoulder, her pointy claws pressed to his eudqi point.

"Kirra, I know you're in there. The evil is possessing you. Don't let it win!" Leon called out.

Zach was dazed by the impact of the claws on his shoulder, but he managed to stand. Mya knew he would swivel away as soon as he saw an opportunity.

He was calling Ciaran on his wrist unit. Mya should have been paying more attention to Kirra, but she'd been distracted by the thought of going to Eudaiz with Zach. Then at that moment, Kirra leaped at Zach from behind. To be fair, she knew it wasn't really Kirra. Elanora's soul had taken Kirra's form. She had warned Zach, but he had been preoccupied. She should have been watching his back. She hadn't done a very good job.

Kirra's eyes flickered. She could see shades of Kirra moving in and out of those eyes. But Elanora was strong, and she had pretty much taken her over. Kirra tried to drag Zach away. Although dazed, Zach stood still and maintained his position.

"Come with me," Elanora spoke from Kirra's body. She pulled at Zach again. He resisted and tried to shrug his shoulder away without success.

"Kirra, be strong! Don't let the evil take over!" Leon cried.

Mya looked at him. She had never seen Leon so emotional. "I don't think she can do that, Leon. She's not strong enough and not equipped for this. She's gone. I'm sorry."

"Let's go, Zach," Elanora said again and pressed Zach's shoulder harder.

"Go my ass!" Zach yanked off his wrist unit, threw it in the air, pulled out his gun, and shot at it. The wrist unit exploded into hundreds of pieces. Mya didn't know how much time Zach had spent playing hologames, but the stunt was impressive. He obviously didn't waste the skills he practiced in the games.

Elanora shrieked in anger. While she was distracted, Zach swiveled away and ducked aside. Even so, Elanora still managed to claw his shoulder.

As soon as Zach got away, Mya roared. A thousand years' worth of her deity power curled into a fireball, and she threw it at Elanora. The fireball expanded like a hot air balloon. She charged forward and grabbed the dagger Zach had dropped on the ground, planning to throw it and pierce Eleanora's heart just like the image of Kirra floating in the fire with the knife through her heart that she had seen in her vision.

Leon flew at Mya, holding her back. "That's enough, Mya. She'll burn to death. That fire will send her to hell. You don't need the dagger."

Mya kicked her legs but couldn't get free of Leon's grip.

Kirra screamed in agony, begging to be let out of the fire.

"Can't you let her go?" Leon asked.

"No, it's not Kirra, Leon. She's gone. That's Elanora. You said so yourself. She's taken other people's forms, so she's more evil than ever now. I have to send her to hell. Let go of me."

"No, Mya, please. Can't you do this for me?"

"Leon, I can't bring Kirra back. I need to check on Zach. Let me go…"

Kirra kept screaming as the fire grew hotter.

They heard a roar. Down the hill behind them charged the black cat. It half ran, half flew and darted straight at the fire. When it got close, it shifted into a man.

"Dex!" Leon gasped.

Dex ran straight into the fireball and snatched Elanora in Kirra's form into his arms. Then there was a small explosion inside the fire. Dex and Elanora dropped into the ground as the soil exploded upward and put out the fire, leaving a big hole in the ground the size of a house.

Mya darted toward Zach and said, "Let me see your back." Before Zach could say anything, she peeled his shirt off and saw that Elanora had missed his eudqi point. The scratch was way below it, and blood was seeping out of the gash. Mya never did like the sight of blood, but it was far better than seeing that silver substance leaking out of him.

They heard a thud. A ball of dirt, grass, and maybe fur appeared. It rolled, expanded, and opened in front of them.

Ciaran scrambled to his feet, still trying to yank his left hand out of the mouth of a leopard. He pulled out his dagger and stabbed until the animal let go. It eased away but peeled off his wrist unit before doing so. Ciaran fell to the ground but stood up instantly and pulled his gun. Before the leopard ran away with his wrist unit in its teeth, he aimed at its head and fired. The head exploded, along with the wrist unit.

"Wow, he's good!" Leon said.

Ciaran whirled around and pointed the gun at Zach.

"Whoa, whoa, it's me! Don't shoot!" Zach said.

Ciaran paused, then he lowered his gun. He glanced around. "This is Earth!" Ciaran said incredulously.

"Yes, and it has been for a long time," Zach said. "This is Mya. That's Leon, my successor." Zach pointed to Ciaran. "And this is Ciaran LeBlanc, king of Eudaiz."

Ciaran nodded in greeting. Or maybe his body just swayed as he tried to regain his balance.

Mya had never seen Ciaran up close. He was magnificent. Striking gray eyes, thick black hair that almost touched his shoulders, the face of a dark angel, and the body of a warrior. He had a tall, lean build and seemed incredibly agile even though, at the moment, he was badly injured. He looked as if he had just battled the entire galaxy.

"You're a mess, Ciaran," Zach said.

"Why don't you try fighting an army of mummies in disguise, a pack of animals whose life mission is to eat me alive, and truckloads of pharaoh lookalikes who think they're gods."

Zach glanced around. "Where are they?"

Ciaran waved his injured hand. "The cat ate my wrist unit. I need to get back to Eudaiz to get to my tower to heal, or I'm going to crash right now. We'll have to use your wrist unit to teleport me."

Zach shook his head. "The cat wanted my wrist unit, too, so I destroyed it."

Ciaran's hands flopped to his sides. He opened his mouth to speak, but before a word could come out of his mouth, he fell face down onto the hot grass.

CHAPTER 20

Elanora opened her eyes and felt the warmth of Dex's body pressed against her. She was lying in his arms. She had no idea it could feel so good. It wasn't the physical contact but rather the sense of safety and the protection that oozed from every muscle in his body and poured into her. Sensing her movement, he released her and put her down on a soft and comfortable surface.

She ached everywhere. She opened her mouth to ask something, but he pressed his thumb gently against her lips. "Hush. You're hurt. Give your body a bit of time to heal."

She could see the ceiling clearly now. Wherever he had brought her felt cozy, like a small cottage in the country. She was lying on a spacious bed. The linen was plain but neat and tidy. The fabric smelled pleasantly earthy. It smelled like...Dex.

She winced and felt the skin on her face crack with the movement.

"Try not to move too much," Dex said and moved away for a moment, out of her sight. He came back quickly with a bowl of liquid. "I had this mixed for you. The shaman I use is really good. This medicine will heal you."

He brought the bowl close to her lips and braced his large hand behind her neck to help her drink. She couldn't move her lips.

"You don't want to take this medicine, or you don't trust me?"

She swallowed a lump in her throat and did her best to open her lips a fraction so that Dex could place the rim of the bowl in a position where she could consume the liquid without choking.

He was right—the medicine was good. The cool liquid ran down her throat, soothing the rough edges. Soon, she could feel the strength coming back to her. Dex sat at the bedside. It was the first chance she'd had to get a good look at him—he was sinfully handsome with a dark aura about him.

The room was so comfortable, and the tranquility in the air made her wish it could last forever. But she knew it wouldn't. She wasn't born to live in peace. This kind of luxury wouldn't last until she had achieved what she had been born and raised to achieve.

"Where are we?"

"My home...I mean, house."

She smiled. "You mean, this is the place you use only to sleep? I can smell the scent of you on this bed."

"You make it sound almost romantic. Yes, I use this bed to sleep."

"What happened?"

He frowned. "You don't remember?"

"Yes, I was trying to stop the car. Zach Flynn and his girls were driving to Sydney, and I stopped them on the road. I borrowed the leopard packs to distract the deity so that I could get Zach and his wrist unit. That's all I remember. But I'm injured now. So that means they beat me up. And you saved my ass."

"Again!" Dex rumbled.

"I'm grateful. I never thanked you for what you've done for me."

"No need. I care about you."

"I guess I'm really messed up this time."

Dex nodded. "Yep. More than you can imagine."

"At least the mess you cleaned up isn't my dead body." She tried to smile, but it still hurt to move the muscles on her face.

Dex chuckled. "Hmmm... What's done is done. I missed this opportunity. But I'll get another one."

"What do you mean?"

"I think you should rest."

"No, tell me. I'm a big girl. You think I can't take it..." She tried to sit up.

"You should rest more."

"I will—if you tell me what I'm missing." She leaned against the headboard and wiped a stray strand of hair from her forehead. Then she looked at her hand.

The hand she was looking at wasn't hers.

She bolted up and scrambled out of the bed. Dex had anticipated her movement and caught her just before she fell to the floor. He scooped her up and put her back down on the bed.

"Let go of me!" She tried to wriggle free.

"If you stay still, I'll tell you what happened."

"I want to see. I want to see my face." She looked down at the body that she could now see wasn't hers.

"You can't go anywhere in your condition. So why don't you stay here and rest, and I'll tell you what happened. Then I'll fetch you a mirror."

She looked into his deep purple eyes and saw his determination. She knew he was right—she was in no shape to go anywhere. She nodded.

"I was on personal business, and I got a call from a client for a job. The job was simple enough that I thought I'd make quick money. All I had to do—in my cat form—was project an image of Zach Flynn to a dimension the client requested. That was it. I was only the messenger."

She nodded. "Do you know the client? Is he from Xiilok?"

"I can't tell you that. But what I can tell you is that when I stepped out from the woods up the hill to capture the image of Zach Flynn, I saw you. I meant you *in this body*!"

Elanora looked at her hands and looked down her body. "This is the girl who was with Mya and Zach! This is *her* body!"

Dex nodded. "Well, I don't know what happened before that or how you got into this form. But when I saw you on that hill, in that woman's form, I froze. I didn't know what to do. The next thing I knew, you were on fire and screaming. So I dropped what I was doing and came to rescue you."

She held his arm and pulled his sleeve up. The skin on his arm had healed, but the faint burn marks were still there. "You got burned as well. You must have run into the fire to get me." A tear ran down her face. Dex wiped it away with his thumb.

"That's okay. I've been through worse. The deity's fire wasn't meant for me, so it couldn't have killed me anyway."

Elanora ground her teeth. "That deity, Mya. That bitch burned me!"

He shrugged. "Because you don't remember how you got into this body, I guess you took the body of other the other woman unintentionally. Maybe because you aren't a pure lynx. In principle, if you intentionally take another body, the deity's fire should have killed you."

She scrambled off the bed. "I've got to take back my body. I'll burn that little deity into ashes."

Dex pulled her back. "You can't. The deity is protected by the power of her Goddess. You're in the wrong here, and no god's going to be on your side."

"She burned me! How can I be on the wrong side? The wrong side of what?"

"One body, one soul. You pushed the other woman's soul out of her body. That's totally unacceptable."

"By the god's laws? Jungle laws? Or were-leopard's laws? I'm sorry, but I have to laugh, Dex. You're a mercenary. You kill for a living. On what multiversal scale does my little body swap compare to what you've done?"

Dex growled. "You don't know what I've done, what I know, or what I can do. My patience is very limited. Now will you sit down, or do I have to tie you up?"

She bared her teeth. "Tie me up if you can." She strode to the door and pushed it open. In front of her was an endless field of tall back grass and weeds. The trees were bare, and their branches reached upward like devil's talons. Above was something that looked like a stormy night sky. But it was shaped like a dome, so she wasn't really sure if it was the sky she was looking at.

She whirled around and saw that Dex had sunk into a comfortable chair. He rested his long legs on a nearby stool. He winked and raised an eyebrow as if waiting for her to say something. When she didn't, he asked, "Need a map?"

"Where are we?"

"The underworld."

She walked back into the room and looked at him. "Who are you, Dex?"

He smiled. "I am the underworld marshal."

"A marshal? You spent so much time with our pack. Who did you want to catch in my leopard pack?"

"You said they weren't your pack."

"That's beside the point..."

He smiled. "Indeed. Look, Elanora, I know you have a lot of questions that I can't answer. But I can tell you this—the fugitives I'm trying to catch have nothing to do with your clan or your pack."

She sat down on a chair and waited for more information. When nothing else came, she asked, "Is that all you're going to tell me?"

He nodded. "In the multiverse, people get killed for pitiful pieces of information. So the less you know, the safer you are."

She was exhausted. She would need more rest and time to digest the information in order to make a decision about the next step. So she walked toward the bed. "I can stay here one more night?"

"Stay as long as you like," he said and stood.

"Where are you going?"

He smiled. "I'm not getting in bed with you. Especially when you're in that body. Get some rest. I'll be back in the morning."

She talked to his back. "You said someone paid you to project the image of Zach Flynn to a dimension you don't know. Was that part of a triangulation process?"

He turned and looked at her, the corner of his lips quirking up. He always had that look when he was intrigued, she thought.

"Indeed. You know about this process. I'm impressed."

"Zach Flynn comes from Eudaiz. He had just communicated with them. I remember it now. I...I mean, this body of mine attacked him when he was talking to someone in Eudaiz. If you were projecting the image of Zach Flynn at the same time to whoever paid you, that person could have used your information to lure the person in Eudaiz to a location of his choice."

Dex grinned. "Now I am *very* impressed. But before you ask, I don't know who it was that my client wanted to capture or which dimension the person in Eudaiz was lured to. But when you were on fire, I dropped the whole process. I don't know what happened afterward."

"The person would be transferred back to the source dimension, which is where Zach Flynn is now."

"Why are you interested in that person?"

"Zach Flynn is a councillor. Whoever he was talking to has to be of a high rank. That person will have the wrist unit I'm after."

"Oh for fuck's sake. There you go about that wrist unit again. Look at yourself in the mirror now and tell me if it's worth it!" He walked out and slammed the door behind him.

CHAPTER 21

Zach rushed toward Ciaran and turned him over. Blood was everywhere. He shook Ciaran's shoulders. He wasn't sure if he'd been hit at his eudqi point or not, but with the injuries he could see, he wasn't sure Ciaran would make it to Eudaiz.

"Ciaran, open your eyes, goddammit. I shouldn't have called you. Don't you die on me."

Ciaran opened his eyes slightly. "Don't flatter yourself. You think I'd jump at your call..."

"Okay, you went to the Babylonian court for vacation and got mugged on the way. Now tell me how to get you back to Eudaiz."

"It was a trap... Someone interfered with your signals..." Ciaran closed his eyes.

"No, no...don't pass out. Tell me what I need to do to get you back to Eudaiz."

"Where are we?"

"Australia."

With his eyes closed, Ciaran said, "Five six five, seven one two, one one nine..." Then he trailed off and said nothing more.

"Hang on for a second!" Zach shouted, but it was too late. Ciaran was totally out of it. "Five six five...then what? Where's your cell phone, Mya?"

Mya thrust her cell phone toward Zach. "It only works on Earth, and in Australia in particular. I haven't had it unlocked for overseas calls. There was one occasion when it worked when I was at the Babylonian court. I don't have an explanation for that one."

Zach looked at Mya and could see she was serious. "I'm not using it to call Eudaiz, Mya. I think Ciaran just gave us the phone number of the Australian branch of LeBlanc Pharmaceuticals."

"The LeBlanc's conglomerate? How will that help?" Mya was astonished.

"I don't have time to explain it now. But it must be a private line. If I can *remember* it. Goddammit, five six five...then what?"

"Don't panic, Zach. I don't sense Ciaran's death. I've just checked my files, and he's not on any of my lists. I know he's king of Eudaiz. But as soon as he lands on Earth, if he's partly human, he would be in my system. Just like you are."

"Are you sure? He's not dead? Not soon? Not..."

"No, Zach. Everyone will die one day, but Ciaran isn't on my list now. Meaning he won't die an unnatural death at this time. Don't let your mind get clogged up with worry. Just call the number."

Zach dialed the number as he remembered it. At the other end of the line, a female voice answered, "Serina's escort service."

"Damn!" Zach hung up. "Five six five...five six five..." he mumbled, his thumb hovering over the keypad of the phone.

"Five six five, seven one two, one one nine," Leon said. Zach and Mya turned and looked at Leon, who had been quiet up until then. Leon shrugged. "If you trust my English, that's what he said."

"Say the number again, please," Zach said and dialed as Leon dictated the number.

Someone at the other end picked up instantly, and a male voice said, "Yes, Ciaran."

Zach cleared his throat. "This is Zach Flynn."

"You're Ciaran's second councillor. What do you need?"

"Ciaran is injured. I need medical assistance."

"How serious?"

"Very. Physical wounds."

"Thank you. I'll dispatch a medical helicopter. Do you need combat assistance?"

"Do you mean fighters?"

"Yes."

"No. Not now. Get the medical assistance first. We're at—"

"I've got your location from the signal of your cell phone. We'll be there as soon as we can."

"Hey, don't you need to verify me? Ciaran has just been ambushed. How secure is your system?"

"Ciaran put this in place. This is the most secure system we can use on Earth. If we get there, and you're not who you say you are, we'll take care of it."

"Like what?"

"We'll kill you."

The line went dead.

Zach looked at the phone and then at Mya. "What the heck just happened?"

"They said they'll kill you if you're not Zach Flynn. So you don't have to worry," Leon answered.

"That was a rhetorical question, Leon."

"And that was a rhetorical answer, Zach."

Zach stood up and growled, "What's your problem, Leon?"

"I don't have a problem. But you do. You sent the bloody leopards to the court. You upset the Goddess and made Mya face even more debts. You called your friend to bring you the jar, and now he's half dead. And you decided to be a gentleman and not kill the black cat up the hill, and it got Kirra!"

"You're mistaken, Leon. When I had to make those decisions to save our asses, you put yourself out there to be meat for those cats. If the animals work up an appetite for you, your meat won't be enough for them. They'll turn on us all. We're in the multiverse, Leon. There is a much bigger picture. Larger things are at stake. Don't think like a pitiful temple guard—"

"Stop bickering you two!" Mya shouted.

They heard a helicopter hovering.

"That was quick!" Zach mumbled.

The helicopter landed, and a search and rescue team stormed out. "That's an Australian search and rescue team," Zach said to Mya through clenched teeth. "They can't be Ciaran's people."

"I didn't think so," Mya agreed.

The leading officer rushed over. "We saw the explosion, sir. Any more casualties?" He pointed at Ciaran.

"No, he's not dead," Zach growled.

The medical team examined Ciaran. "He's alive!" a doctor shouted out to the officer. "We'll airlift him to emergency."

The officer turned toward Zach. "Who's his next of kin?"

"Me," Zach said.

"Please follow me, sir."

They loaded Ciaran onto the helicopter.

"She's my wife. Can she come with us?" Zach pointed at Mya.

"Yes, sir, we can take one more on the chopper. The road rescue will be here in a minute." The officer looked at Leon, who was standing at a distance and looking at the helicopter with suspicion.

Zach looked at Leon and rolled his eyes. "That's my brother. He has a special condition and can't be left alone."

The officer frowned. "All right. Come on in." He turned and asked another officer to stay behind. The helicopter took off. Leon looked as if he would sink into the seat if he could. His hands gripped the edge of the seat tightly. He dared not close his eyes, and he was sweating profusely. Zach figured his successor had not only never been on a chopper before but had probably not even imagined something like it even existed. He squeezed Mya's hand and nodded toward Leon. Mya got the hint. She moved closer to Leon to give him a bit of comfort.

Zach turned toward the doctor who was working on Ciaran. "Is he going to be okay?"

"I'm not sure. We have to get to the hospital to know for sure. He's sustained some very serious injuries. A lot of them don't look like they were caused by the explosion that made that gigantic hole in the ground. What happened?"

Zach shook his head. "Don't know. We were hiking, and he was standing right next to where the explosion happened." Out of the corner of his eyes, Zach thought he saw a second helicopter hovering in the sky. It looked as if it was hiding among the clouds, but Zach had seen this technology in the transitional zone of the multiverse. The cloud lookalike created a dimensional reflective shield that blinded its foes.

Trained Eudaizian soldiers could see it. Some Xiilok fighters could as well. But he didn't think ordinary human eyes would be able to see the combat helicopter that was about to gun them down.

"Shit!" he muttered.

Zach turned to warn Mya, and as he did, they felt the impact of the first blast at their own helicopter.

PART TWO

CHAPTER 22

Mya surged up to her feet quickly when the helicopter dipped and quickly regained her balance. Zach held onto her, but when he figured she was fine, he released her arms and rushed over to Ciaran. The pilot swore and tried to calm the medical team.

When Mya followed Zach, he turned and said, "They didn't shoot us with live ammunition. I think they want to capture us." He then searched Ciaran's jacket pockets.

"The jar isn't with Ciaran, if that's what you're after," she said. "I can't sense it. It's not here."

Zach nodded and stopped searching.

"What the hell! Where did they come from?" the pilot exclaimed.

The other helicopter had lowered its dimensional shield, and it hovered right in front of their own. It radioed the pilot and asked him to land.

"That chopper is military grade. You'd better do what they say," Zach said.

As soon as they landed their helicopter, a group of men in military uniform approached from the other aircraft. The closer they came, the louder the alarm bells rang in Mya's mind. She wasn't alarmed because a bunch of armed men were approaching them, but she was definitely alarmed by their aura. She had fought them before when she was still with the court.

They were dressed in modern clothing, but she knew they didn't belong to this time—or this world. "They're from another world, Zach," she said.

He nodded and slid his hand toward his gun. From the corner of her eye, she could see Leon had readied his hand on the hilt of his knife.

"Don't..." she told them both. "Too many civilians, and Ciaran can't protect himself." But before she could say anything more, the men pulled their guns and sprayed bullets in their direction.

Zach pulled Mya down and slammed the helicopter's door closed with Ciaran inside. Leon lay flat on the ground, cursing when a bullet hit his shoulder. All the medical staff and the pilot dropped dead on the ground.

Zach cursed. "Bastards! They probably think Ciaran has the jar." From the ground, Zach took out a couple of men. But Mya knew they were out numbered. The men kept approaching. Zach stood up and raised his hands in the air. "I've got something you want."

The men stopped. The one who appeared to be the leader pulled his mask up. They could see his irises were filled with swimming worms. Zach asked softly, "Do you think we can take them?"

"Sure," Leon said immediately.

Mya looked at them again. They had been Xiilok fighters since the ancient time. There were eight men. If they put their guns away, between Zach, Leon, and herself, they could take the men down—*if* things went smoothly. The men might have military training, but her scuffling skills weren't bad. Zach was good, and Leon was exceptionally good. She nodded to Zach.

"You're looking for a jar, right?" Zach said to the man.

"Yes," was the man's response.

"I have it! Don't shoot," Zach said.

The group lowered their guns and approached.

Aren't you stupid? You should have asked Zach to show the jar. Now...come closer, Mya thought.

The men had moved about twenty feet closer to them when their heads and bodies exploded with laser beams. A short distance away, they could see a couple of jeeps speeding closer.

"That's Ciaran's people," Zach said to Mya.

"Are you sure?" Mya asked.

"Let me check." Zach narrowed his eyes. Mya knew he was sending sound waves at the men. If had spoken to one of them, and they claimed they knew who he was, and that sound being was his unique talent. If they were Ciaran's men, they should have appropriate reaction reaching his sound waves.

The man leading the group nodded at Zach, signaling he had received the sound signals.

Mya felt a prick at the back of her neck, and her alarm bells began to ring again. It was the same feeling she'd had with the armed group they had just killed. "Are you sure, Zach? These are ancient soldiers. They're creatures. Are you sure Ciaran used them and stationed them on Earth?" she asked Zach between her teeth.

"No, I'm not. But there's no way they knew the number Ciaran set up."

"What if they killed Ciaran's men those talked to you. Or they interfered the signals such as those they have just killed. The only one who can tell us now is Ciaran. And you told them Ciaran is out."

Zach nodded. "You're right. Ciaran has to be injured bad enough so that I had to call on his behalf. Then no one can verify these guys. Either they come for the jar or for Ciaran, they're bad news. Any idea of how to get us all out of here in one piece?"

Mya shook her head.

"Why don't we go back to the court?" Leon quietly said.

Mya and Zach turned to look at Leon. Mya grinned. "I love you, Leon!"

Zach frowned. "But Ciaran said Babylon was a trap. They ambushed him."

"Not at the court. He must have been somewhere else," Leon said.

"Also, genuine Babylonian soldiers don't look like the mummies or pharaohs. that injured him. He was somewhere else, Zach," she said.

He nodded. "If they were capable of intercepting his signal, then they would have no problem manipulating a dimensional shift to change his destination."

Zach turned back quickly, smiled at the approaching group of men, and gestured toward the helicopter. The man nodded, acknowledging Zach's invitation.

"What exactly do I need to do, Mya?" Zach asked quietly. I don't have my wrist unit anymore. We can't teleport off."

Mya smiled. "Follow us." She winked at Leon, and they opened the helicopter's door and quickly climbed inside.

The armed men were ten feet away.

Mya left the door open so they could see Ciaran inside. She grabbed Ciaran's hand with one hand and Zach's hand with the other. "Close your eyes," she said quickly. Leon stepped in, grabbing Ciaran's hand and Zach's hand, closing the circle. Zach closed his eyes.

Mya channeled to the Babylonian court the way she always did. The last time, she had accidentally taken her cell phone with her, and it worked. This time, she deliberately willed her minor deity power in her mind to take any subject she had in contact to the court.

She hoped it worked just as well.

CHAPTER 23

Kirra ran aimlessly through the black forest. Bare, coal-colored tree trunks growing from the muddy ground looked like the devil's hands reaching for her. She didn't know where she was or why and from what she was running.

The last thing she remembered was a sensation of weightlessness. It was as if her soul had been vacuumed out of herself so quickly she could feel the empty hole it created in her mind. Her body seemed to weigh a ton. She tripped on uneven ground and fell in front of a puddle. She looked at the reflection of herself in the dark water. Her hair was tattered and singed at the ends. Although there were signs of healing, she could see the burns on her face.

Then she remembered the incident when her consciousness went in and out. She had been in the middle of a fire, burning like a torch. Outside the fire, Leon, Mya, and Zach stood looking at her in helplessness.

Leon looked devastated. She recalled he was begging her to stay. *I didn't mean to go anywhere, Leon. Why were you so desperate? Why was I on fire?*

"Elanora," a voice said from behind her. She whirled around, prepared to put up a fight. She vaguely remembered the lynx Elanora and the way she had attacked them in both animal and human form. She remembered stabbing the lynx in Elanora form to death.

The man in front of her looked familiar—tall, strong, with a dark aura around him. His eyes were the most familiar feature. Dark eyes with a shade of purple. *Who is he?* He didn't look as if he wanted to harm her. But why had he called her Elanora?

The man approached. "I know you think you're invincible. But let me tell you, there is no mercy in this underworld. You aren't meant to be here, especially in the form of that woman. If you get caught, there is nothing I can do for you."

So this is the underworld? All right...does that mean she might be dead? "I'm dead. Why do I care if I get caught?" she asked.

"You're not dead. I told you that. You've lost your body. But I'll figure something out for you. If you take the potion I fixed for you, it won't be long until this body is fit and healthy so you can return the body back to the woman you took it from. If you stay in the house during the process, it will be best for both of us."

She nodded.

He arched an eyebrow at her obedience. He approached and tilted her chin up. "You know what? If you had just agreed with whatever I said and behaved sensibly—as you are now—your life would have been a lot easier. Just stay at home and be safe. You don't have to live up to whatever elusive mission someone heaped on you."

She smiled.

He smiled back. The care in his eyes was convincing. It reminded her of Zach. She shook the thought out of her mind.

"What?" he asked.

"What's what?"

"Why did you shake your head?"

"Oh, nothing. Bad memories."

He embraced her. "I'm sorry you have to go through this. I know it hurt. But we'll get through this together."

"How can we return this body back to the woman? Isn't she dead?"

The man shook his head. "I don't know. Let's go home. I'll get more information and see what I can do. But before we figure this out, promise me you won't run away like this again?"

She nodded and followed him. He wrapped his large arm around her shoulders. For a moment, she almost felt safe.

CHAPTER 24

Mya felt a thud, and the transport came to a stop. She opened her eyes and saw that Leon and Zach had opened theirs as well. Ciaran was still unconscious on the stretcher. And they were still in the helicopter. But outside the window of the helicopter was a totally different vista from the Australian outback they had just left. So they *had* channeled elsewhere—including everyone and the entire helicopter! As to where they currently were, she had no idea.

Without looking outside, Leon said, "This is not the court."

"How did this happen? We channeled the same way every single time between the court and earth," Mya said.

Leon rubbed his hand on his shoulder where the bullet had hit him earlier. "It healed!" he gasped.

"Look at Ciaran!" Zach said in disbelief.

On the stretcher, although there was still blood everywhere, Ciaran's visible injuries healed in front of their very eyes.

The helicopter shook as if it was about to takeoff. Mya braced her hands on the floor. "It's not me!"

"I'm not doing anything, either," Leon said, sitting on the floor, bracing himself against the chair.

Zach hung on to the stretcher as it slid toward the door. He kicked the door closed. The helicopter lifted off the ground and zoomed ahead as if they were in a Eudaizian spaceship.

Outside the window, objects flew past at incredible speeds. Too fast for them to recognize anything. In a short while, they landed violently. Everything was still. It was dark and quiet both inside and outside the helicopter. So quiet they could hear themselves breathing.

"Can we move now?" Leon asked.

"Yes, and can someone unstrap me, please?" Ciaran said.

"Ciaran? Are you okay?" Zach said as he searched for the buckles in the dark.

"They should be along the side. Stop touching everywhere, Zach. You're weirding me out," Ciaran said.

Mya let out a small laugh, imagining the scene. They heard the snapping sound of the buckles and the sound of the stretcher moving as Ciaran sat up. "Where are we?" he asked.

"Inside a chopper. That's the only thing we're sure of at the moment," Zach said.

"All right. Let's get some light," Ciaran said and worked his way toward the cockpit.

"How?" Mya asked.

"He can drive anything with wheels and an engine on Earth and anything that flies in Eudaiz. I think turning on a light is a trivial matter," Zach said.

"Thanks, Zach, but I think I can speak for myself," Ciaran said as the light came on. He came back from the cockpit and sat down.

Wow, what a scene he makes. Something about him is so masculine and powerful. It draws people in. With Zach, any female who looks at him for more than two seconds has to cross their legs because he stirs up their vital part so uncontrollably. But with Ciaran, females just dive in like a moth to a flame, Mya thought.

"Hello again, Mya, Leon. I don't know what's going on just yet, but I guess I should thank you for saving me," Ciaran said, glancing down at his arms and his body. "The blood on my clothes could scare young children. But for some magical reason, I think I'm completely free of injuries. Can you tell me what happened?"

Zach chuckled and looked at Mya. "Naturally, he wants a full report."

Ciaran smiled. "A short one will do for now."

Leon said, "You were out. A bunch of doctors came and packed you into this big bird. Then some men came along in another big bird and killed the doctors. Then some different men came and killed the killers. Zach and Mya thought we should run before they killed us, so we channeled back to the court."

Mya smiled. "Leon has never seen or been on a helicopter before."

"Big bird is an accurate description," Ciaran said. "So we're at the Babylonian court?"

Zach shook his head. "We know you thought Babylon was a trap, but Mya and Leon said the men you fought didn't sound like Babylonian soldiers. So Mya and Leon channeled us back here—I mean, back to the court."

Ciaran nodded and looked at Mya and Leon. "I understand. Not all creatures can travel across the multiverse. So back and forth between the court and Earth is your usual route?"

"Are we *creatures*?" Leon asked in astonishment.

"I used to differentiate between humans and other creatures. But having seen the multiverse, every being is a creatures to me now."

Leon grinned. "I can tell the Goddess that she's only a creature."

Mya pushed at Leon's shoulder.

Zach shook his head. "I called the number you gave me. The search and rescue team came first. Then Xiilok fighters. They killed the medical team. Then some guys I thought were *your* guys came and killed the Xiiloks. We ran before they approached us, so we can't verify them. But Mya said they were ancient creatures. Any idea what happened, Ciaran?"

Ciaran leaned back in his seat. "The station I planted in Australia is operated by humans. They might use fighters from the multiverse, but they work for me."

"So the guys approaching us might have been your guys?" Zach asked.

"Not necessarily. They could be mercenaries from the multiverse. Given that the ones who ambushed me intercepted your signals, I have no doubt they'd do it again. Until I talk to the station to verify, we can't draw any conclusions."

"How do you talk to your station? You don't have your wrist unit. I don't know where we are now, but I'm sure we aren't on Earth," Mya said.

"Let's take a look outside," Ciaran said and reached for the handle to open the door to go outside. Something white smashed into the window. He jerked back. The thing outside looked like a ghost, if indeed the was any good theory about what a ghost should look like. A fair description would be a human shape with hollow eyes as if wearing a mask with a soft white material draped over it, floating in the air.

The thing stuck on the window for a short moment then slid down, leaving a slimy smear on the glass.

CHAPTER 25

Richard poured the contents of the wooden box out and picked up the object that he thought was an innocent necklace charm. It was a talisman—crafted in shiny black metal. "This represents your promise? Do you realize how that sounds?"

Casey sighed. "I told you that you weren't ready for the truth"

"I am. But this is not the truth. Do you think I'm stupid?"

"No..."

"Then tell me something other than you're a soul trader and floating through one life after another is what you're supposed to do. If that's true, there was no reason for your son to get so upset in the hospital. He almost killed me." He whirled around. "I can't see you right now, but I know when you're lying."

"Richard..."

"I know your situation is strange, but the laws of logic and harmony are relevant anywhere, in any world, Casey. If it was your normal cycle that you're expect to die because of that falling rail, and you didn't, it ought to upset something. And because I interfered with your faith, and you traded a soul for me, and you actually didn't die as you had other times, then some cycle must have been seriously broken. That was why your son was upset."

"Dex always disagreed with what I do. And you're right. I broke the cycle, and I have to face the consequences. There is nothing you or Dex can do for me now."

"I don't believe you. If there is a question, there has to be an answer. And saying there's no solution isn't an answer. It's an acceptance of defeat. If you don't point me in the right direction, I'll just have to do it by trial and error. But first, I'll keep this talisman."

"Oh no, please give it to Dex."

"If it's a very important object as you've said, why is it safer with him than with me?"

"Please, Richard. You're a human. The less you know, the better it is …"

"Hell with being human. Hell to all this, Casey. You tangled me up in this mess, and you can't just push me out now."

"You pushed me out of the way of that rail. You interrupted my life…and my death. I want you out. I am immortal. You're a mortal. We have no future together, Richard. Just go away…"

He glanced around the room and nodded. "All right. I will." He turned to walk away.

"Please leave the talisman. Dex will come here for it."

He turned around and opened his palm. "Take it yourself." He waited. He hoped she would appear so that he could see her for the last time. There was no movement. It was silent.

"Casey, if you don't take it, I'll keep it. If it's that important, I can't leave it lying around.

He heard a snapping sound like electric current, and then the flickering image of Casey appeared in front of him. The sadness and hollowness in her eyes stabbed at his heart. He recoiled and stepped backward.

"Have I caused you that much pain, Casey? I'm sorry..." Although her image was flickering, he could see tears rolling down her face. "Please don't cry. You can have your talisman back. I can give it to Dex. I shouldn't leave it lying around."

"Thank you..." she sobbed.

"Please don't cry." He reached his hand out, wanting to touch her face. His hand went right through her image.

She cried even harder. "You see, I don't even have a form now..."

"It has to be my fault. Tell me how to fix it, Casey. What do you need? Please. Yes, I'm a mortal. If I have to die because of this, so be it. Everyone dies. Don't you think I was prepared for that when I pushed you out of the way of the falling rail?"

"Please stop talking, Richard."

"Casey, as a human, I've lived long enough to know the consequences of my actions. I loved my late wife. And I love my daughter. I have a life. I know what I am doing. Why do you think I pushed you away from that rail?

"No, no...stop talking, Richard!"

"What are you afraid I'm going to say?"

"Don't, Richard."

"I love you, Casey Anderson." A burning sensation punched through his palm. "Ouch," he grunted and stifled a curse. The talisman had branded his palm. He jerked his hand back, dropping the talisman onto the floor. On the ground, it looked like a cold piece of metal, but when he looked as his palm, he could see his flesh was still sizzling with the unwanted tattoo.

CHAPTER 26

Dex landed on the soft ground outside the Babylonian court. He had been here a few times, and he'd hated every second of it. He preferred his underworld—a place that bore the stigma of housing evils. What people didn't know was that the underworld was just like any other world and had its own rules and regulations. Creatures had to comply with the rules to live there. He was a marshal of the underworld, hunting down a fugitive of centuries. As cynical as it might sound, if he was the one to enforce the law in an evil world, did that make his fugitive a good guy by common mortal standards?

He shook his head. He was overthinking, as always. He focused on a small door leading to a small chamber in the basement of the Well of Death. This was where the court held criminals who were to be executed, sentencing them to be eaten by all sorts of creatures the Goddess had captured. She used this execution as a form of entertainment.

Dex shook his head. Having seen much brutality in the multiverse and in his line of work, he still shuddered as he thought about Ishtar's tastes in entertainment.

His contact had left a small candle by the window. It was a welcoming sign. He pushed the door open and walked in. But instead of seeing his usual informant, a small creature he had recruited from the underworld, he saw Ishtar sitting graciously on a chair. Her commanders flanked her, weapons drawn.

He didn't attempt to withdraw because he knew they had covered the exit. He could see body parts and a bloody pool on the floor. He didn't need to ask—he knew they were the remains of his informant.

"What kind of marshal has the name Dex?" Ishtar's voice rang out like a bell.

"My full name is Dexonysus The Fifth Alaxamdro, my Goddess. As you can see, it's a little complicated and not too efficient when I operate in the field."

Ishtar smiled. "That is a fair answer. Now who or what is the fugitive you and your underworld are after in my world? Before you answer, your informant is an example of what happens when I'm given an answer I'm not pleased with."

"I cannot name the fugitive, my Goddess. But I must clarify that I have been hunting him for centuries across multiple worlds, not just yours. You shouldn't take that as an offense."

She smiled. "That's an answer I'm not pleased with." She flicked her fingers, and the commanders by her side charged at him. Dex knew he had a physical advantage. But in this confined space, his size might prove to be a disadvantage.

He drew his double knives—the primitive weapons that were most reliable in any dimension in the multiverse. He took down the two commanders before he felt the sharp pain of a blade penetrating his back. He swung his knife around and cut a head right off. He had no idea to whom that head belonged.

His world started to blur.

He slammed a hard kick at another commander who stood by the door and stormed out.

He ran as fast as he could in the darkness, knowing he needed only to reach his exit point. Once there, he could transport himself back to his home, his underworld. Sprinting hard, he crashed into a concrete wall, seeing a thousand stars as he fell.

Dex scrambled up to his feet. It wasn't a wall he had just run into—it was Ishtar's shield, coasted by her Goddess's power. Ishtar stood with a smirk on her face. She had lived up to her reputation, Dex thought. Her face glowed in satisfaction at the pain he suffered.

"I'm authorized to hunt this fugitive in the multiverse. I am protected by the multiversal agreement. You don't want to hurt me, Ishtar."

She laughed. "Nice bluff, Dex. If there is such an agreement, the multiverse might be at peace at some point. But Dex, I know you're a rogue. You're a marshal by contract..."

"But before the contract finishes, I am protected by the gods of the underworld."

"Who happens to be my longtime acquaintance." She swung her arms, and he found himself thrown several feet into the air and smashed down hard on the ground like a rag doll.

He knew she was telling the truth. She knew people in high places in the underworld. But he didn't have a choice. He had to stand his ground. From the corner of his eye, he saw how close he was to the exit point. It had taken him centuries to build those exit points between worlds, and not everyone knew them. Once he got back to the underworld, Ishtar wouldn't be able to find him.

As she had said, he was a rogue marshal.

Dex let his body roll on the rocky ground for a little longer than he needed to. He pulled himself up slowly, trying to appear as if he was in more pain than he actually was. Ishtar fed on the pain of others. She looked pleased.

When the time was right, he shot up and darted toward his exit point. But Ishtar was faster. Her arms stretched out, and she grabbed at him from behind. When he fell, her steely arms dragged him and pressed him down to the ground as hard as she could to maximize the damage.

He could feel his skin peeling off.

He could shift into his cat form. Maybe by doing so, he could slide out of her grip. She must have read his mind because her giant hand grabbed him by the neck. She pressed against it. He could feel her thumb imprinted against the back of his head. She was immobilizing him. She knew about his poisonous gland. She knew he could release it and use it like venom to paralyze people.

She was pressing against it to force the release of the venom into his own body.

He wriggled hard, but he knew it wouldn't work. His body started to feel numb. He summoned whatever remaining strength he had and said, "Nunnaki."

"What?"

As Ishtar growled, her hand loosened a bit.

"Nunnaki didn't die," he continued.

"What did you say?"

Her hand loosened its grip on his head. Taking the opportunity, he threw a smoke bomb at her and jumped into his exit point. Into whatever was on the other side. He didn't care as long as he was no longer in Babylon and no longer held captive by Ishtar. He'd do whatever it took.

He landed in his familiar underworld and reeled home. He could see Elanora in Kirra's form in the distance, waiting for him at the door. A scene every man longed for! He tried to make it with all the stamina he had left. And then he couldn't remember anything else.

CHAPTER 27

Mya watched Ciaran push everyone back from the door while he stared at the slimy smear on the glass. He leaned forward, trying to hear if there was any unusual sound outside. She smiled to herself and wondered what Ciaran would do if he were in her position. Hell, she didn't want to think about what she would do if she were in his position, having to protect a universe of hundreds of millions of citizens.

"Instead of trying to listen for something outside, why don't I just do a wipe with my sound waves?" Zach asked.

Ciaran waved his hand absently. "You're right. Sorry. Go ahead."

Mya had a theory about the flying white object, but she figured she'd give the male species an opportunity to do their job. After more than a thousand years doing her job, she knew holding off a little and letting men do their thing could save her a lot of unnecessary debate.

"Anything?" Ciaran asked, raising an eyebrow.

"There isn't anything moving out there," Zach said.

"Okay, let's go then," Ciaran said impatiently and pulled the door open. As soon as it opened, another white object flew toward them. He slammed the door closed, and the glass copped another slimy mark. He turned toward Zach and glared.

"I meant to say there isn't anything *alive* moving out there. Whatever that thing is, it isn't alive. Look, Ciaran, we're on the same boat here. We all want to go home. But can we try not to rush things?" Zach said.

"I'm not rushing anything," Ciaran growled and pulled the door open again. Another white object flew toward the door. In anticipation, he pulled his gun and fired. The laser beam hit the object. They heard a quack, and it exploded into thousands of shiny floating particles which quickly dissolved into thin air.

"You've just killed a ghost!" Mya said.

Another object flew toward them, copping Ciaran's beam, and then disappeared.

"I think they like the light," Leon said.

Zach darted toward the cockpit and turned off the light. The door of the helicopter was still open, but there were no white objects flying toward them.

"Good guess, Leon," Zach said.

"It wasn't a guess. It's common knowledge where we come from—lost spirits are attracted to light," Mya said. "It's okay to go outside now. I think I know where we are." To her surprise, Ciaran asked no questions. Even before she ended her sentence, he walked right outside. Either he trusted her judgment, or he couldn't wait to get the hell out of there. She leaned toward the latter for a plausible explanation.

Zach glanced back at her, and she could see he was thinking the same thing. He followed Ciaran outside, and Leon went after him. Then she stepped out. The scene in front of her hit her like a tidal wave—a memory of a scene of death and the remnants of her battle in the valley that had cost more than two thousand lives.

She gasped and staggered back as she felt Zach wrap his arm around her. "Are you okay?" he asked. "They're just flying around. They're not attacking us." He pushed her behind him.

She shook her head, snapping herself back to what she considered to be their current reality. Floating in front of them were groups of the human-shaped white objects with hollow eyes. "They're spirits. We're at the market of souls and spirits."

Zach raised an eyebrow. "Why the hell are we here?"

"Can these spirits be considered creatures, Mya? Can they harm us or any other living creatures?" Ciaran asked.

"No, they're lost spirits. They've been taken by soul traders, but their souls have not been exchanged. So they're lost. Most of the time, it happens with unnatural deaths."

"So are we where you think we are?" Zach asked.

"We're not in Babylon. Leon and I channeled us to the court, but somehow we ended up here."

"But is this a place? If I could navigate, I could fly us home in that chopper," Ciaran said as he looked up to the black sky. But there was nothing around them. It looked and felt like a cemetery even though there were no tombs around. It was simply a dark, flat, black surface without any landmarks he could use for navigation.

Agitated, Ciaran walked back and forth. Mya looked at Zach, and he looked back at her and shook his head. He whispered into her ear, "I've never seen him like this before. He has a temper, but he's always in control and never loses his cool. This agitation isn't like Ciaran at all."

"Ciaran," Leon called out.

Ciaran stopped pacing. "Yes?"

"These two wonder why you're agitated."

Mya glared at Leon. He shrugged.

Ciaran stared at them for a short moment and then sighed. "I had a disagreement with Madeline. I wasn't focused. When you called, and the call was interrupted, I knew the signal might not be authentic, but I didn't check it. I left without having a word with Madeline. I left a message for her. But now that I think about it, that message might have been intercepted as well. Whoever paid for my head probably wanted my family, too. My wife and children might be in trouble. And now, without the wrist unit, I have no idea how to contact her to let her know. I'm not psychic. I can't channel!" He waved his arms in the air in frustration and then let them flop at his sides.

"Look out!" Leon shouted and pointed.

Behind Ciaran, the lost spirits gathered and lined up. They turned and looked as if they were going to fly right at him.

"Mya, you said they're spirits, right? They won't bite?" Zach asked.

"In theory, they can't."

"What would make them attack?" Ciaran asked.

Mya shuddered at her thought. "They might if they were offered a chance to be traded by a soul trader."

"Some traders make these lost souls feel wanted. What scumbags! Trading for what?" Ciaran muttered to himself.

"If they come all at once, we'll be in deep shit," Zach said. He pulled out his gun and pushed Mya behind him. She yanked him back by his jacket. "I'm sick of you trying to protect me. This is my turf. I'll call the shots here." She pointed at Ciaran. "You as well, Ciaran. Get back here."

"I beg your pardon?"

"I said get back here, Ciaran. Leon and I will handle this. In this world, your technology and your supernatural skills don't seem to do much."

Ciaran stood still. "You expect me to go back there and behave like a meek dog?"

"I'm sorry if I hurt your ego, Ciaran. But I'm a deity. I'm in charge here." As she ignored Zach's curses and darted past Ciaran, the flock of spirits formed into the shape of a spear and were about to attack. She knew Leon was right behind her. She had fought many battles, but she'd never fought spirits. *If they're dead already, can she kill them again?* she wondered.

She shook the thought out of her mind. Curling her hand into a fist, she willed her minor deity power. In her mind, she aimed at the bad spirits, whom she was entitled to kill. She threw her fireballs, hoping the majority of those in the way were bad spirits.

The fire hit a number of them, and they exploded into nothingness. A loud quacking sound disturbed the quietness of the market. The wind started to whirl up, and they heard the hum and chant echoed as if from the underworld.

She shifted her shoulders. She had taken out half of the flock. Those remaining were not bad spirits, and that was why they hadn't been killed. But if they had accepted bribes from a soul trader and attacked them—people whom they shouldn't attack—she thought they should be considered bad spirits. Apparently, she was wrong. Again.

The spirits formed again in the sky, this time as an arrow. But now, they were not only lost spirits, they were also angry ones because she had attacked them first.

"My fire can't kill them. How many can your guns take out?" she asked, turning her head slightly toward the back, expecting an answer from Zach and Ciaran. But she heard neither.

"Hello? I need back up here!" she repeated as the angry spirits took aim and were about to fly at them.

CHAPTER 28

Ciaran was sure it was enough justification for him to do what he had just done. Mya had called for help. In his panicked state, Zach was quick enough to let him know that Mya couldn't kill the good spirits. Yes, they were angry spirits, but they weren't sinful ones, so her power wouldn't work on them.

While Mya's power was selective, Ciaran's wasn't. His mind blade didn't discriminate. It was a powerful weapon, and it did one job—it killed whomever or whatever he wanted it to.

He conjured the fury in his mind and shaped up a gigantic steel blade that hurled through the air at the flock of angry spirits. The blade spun and swung, dipping and descending on them from above. A quacking, squealing, and crying sound flooded the air of whatever the place was they were.

Soon, the spirits disappeared into nothingness.

The blade dug a large hole in the ground and gradually cracked open the area so it looked like the Grand Canyon.

The execution sucked energy from Ciaran and weakened him. He felt Zach dragging him back by the shoulders. "That's enough, Ciaran."

He shrugged Zach off. "I didn't get all of them..."

Zach grabbed him again. "Just a handful. Let them go. They're fleeing the market."

Ciaran looked up. Zach was right. He never attacked a runaway man. Suddenly, a sharp pain stabbed in his head. He grabbed it with his hands. He had been attacked like this once during his fight to the coronation. Creatures in the cosmos always tried to attack his mind—every power-hungry creature wanted a piece of his mind.

Ciaran clenched his teeth and willed against the suction of whatever stabbed at his mind right now. A thought dawned on him. This was a trap. For him. Someone or something wanted him to open his mind and attack the spirits. He grunted in pain as he tried to resist the pull. A drop of blood trickled down his nose.

"Talk to me, Ciaran. What's happening? What do you want me to do?" Zach asked.

Ciaran found himself speechless. The agony intensified. "Let's get out of here," he said through his teeth. We need to get back to the helicopter, and I'll fly us out of here."

Zach helped him walk and said, "I certainly trust your sense of direction. You said before that you can't navigate out of here. But as long as we don't hit hard objects, I'm fine with it."

They heard a quacking sound in the distance. It was a mourful sound, hovering eerily in the air.

Ciaran's knees buckled.

"Come on, Ciaran." Zach pulled him up.

Mya rushed over. "They're after you, Ciaran."

"Yes, but I don't know what they want. I don't have the jar with me."

Mya shook her head. "I don't think this is about the jar at all. I didn't channel us here. Your mind did."

"Do you mean Ciaran wanted us to come here?" Leon asked.

"Your bullet wound was healed on the way here, remember, Leon?" Mya said. "Ciaran's injuries were a lot more serious. His mind wanted to heal him, and it channeled us through a healing area."

"Well then, why is he hurting now?" Zach asked.

"Ciaran, please look at me," Mya said.

He looked into her dark, intense eyes.

She said, "I think your mind or someone or something that has to do with your mind wants to heal you."

"Heal me by sucking my brain out?" Ciaran growled.

"It's not your brain. Or even your mind." She looked into his eyes. "I think they want your soul. This is the soul trading market. We're here for a reason. And that reason is you."

He wanted to chuckle, but it was too painful to do so. He shook his head. "Okay, so if someone wants my soul, why not just kill me? Why take me through the healing process? Letting me die would be more convenient."

Mya stared straight into his eyes and stayed firm. "That someone might have tried while ambushing you. But apparently it wasn't successful. So they tried again. Ciaran, have you ever dealt with a soul trader?"

"What?"

"You heard me."

Zach nodded. "He heard you, and he's plotting a lie right now."

"You know nothing, Zach," Ciaran snarled.

"I'm not blind. During your coronation, when you got bitten in the heart by that cobra, I saw you die. How did you get back up? And I heard Madeline thanking someone."

Ciaran shoved Zach's shoulder and stood up. "It's none of your business."

"The hell it's not. Your mind brought us here. Now, if you're going cuckoo, how are we supposed to get back?" Zach snapped back.

"There's one way to find out, Ciaran," Mya said. "Let me look into your soul."

"I beg your pardon?"

"I can see if it's your soul they want."

"If they want my corrupted soul, what can you do, Mya? The answer to your request is no." Ciaran staggered back as Mya approached him. He was feeling weaker by the second, but he wouldn't give in to this. "You don't have my permission, Mya,"

He felt a hard blow on the back of his head, and his world went blank for a brief moment.

Then he was floating. He saw himself lying on the ground.

"Why did you do that, Leon?" Zach shouted.

Leon was standing over him and had apparently just hit him on the head. "You all took too long to talk to him. And he wasn't going to agree to what you asked for anyway. If we want to get out of here, we're going to have to let Mya do her magic. I can't help with that, and we need to pay attention to that fact," Leon ranted. Then he pointed in the distance.

They looked up at the distant horizon and saw the shape of a woman rising from the ground. She wore a white dress, her long hair was as white as the clouds, and her eyes sparkled in a shade of fiery red. Her shape grew larger by the second.

"What is it, Mya?" Zach asked.

"I don't know yet." She quickly turned toward Ciaran, who still lay on the ground.

Ciaran frowned at the floating image of himself. *Is this my soul? Why am I outside my body?* "Let me talk to the woman," he said out loud, but no one seemed to be able to hear him.

On the ground, Mya rushed over to his body, hovered her hands over his head, and closed her eyes. Ciaran looked up and saw that the floating woman had risen as high as a small hill. Zach stood next to Mya. Ciaran understood Zach had to protect both his motionless body on the ground and Mya while she was doing her job, whatever that was.

Leon stepped forward and away, facing the giant woman. "What are you going to do, Leon? Stab her with your little knives?" Ciaran asked, knowing Leon couldn't hear him. But he admired the man's courage.

Ciaran looked at the woman. "I wager you can hear me."

She looked at him and smiled. "Yes. Clearly." Ciaran didn't know what Death sound like, but he thought her hollow voice could be a close match.

Leon frowned and turned around, looking behind him and above. He had obviously seen the woman talking to someone behind him, but he couldn't see who it was and couldn't hear the conversation.

Mya gasped and withdrew, staggering back on the ground, falling on her backside. Zach grabbed her. "What did you see, Mya?"

She whispered into Zach's ears, but Ciaran could hear her because he stood right next to them. "There are two souls. I saw two in Ciaran."

Ciaran felt a pull and knew that his body on the ground had started to wake and he would be sucked back in. He looked at the woman at the distance. "You're a soul trader. And you want my soul. Why?"

She raised an eyebrow. "Who wouldn't want a king's spirit? It's been damaged. But you did well to preserve it, and so I'll take it."

Ciaran smiled. "But you can't trade my soul as you usually do. Am I correct?"

The woman smiled again. "You are knowledgeable. Yes, your soul has been sealed. I need the opening spell."

"And you think I will voluntarily give you the spell so that you can take my soul?"

"It's a fair trade. You have more than one in you. I only want the king's spirit."

"What do I get in return?"

"Your son."

Even disembodied, Ciaran felt his knees weaken in the flickering image of his soul. He couldn't find a response.

The woman smiled again. "You see, you'll live. You don't need that king's spirit. You don't have to carry it. It's not your duty. But you only have one son, and he's a mere infant. I can't make an appreciable profit from him, but losing him would be a huge loss to you, wouldn't it?"

"If you know I have the king's spirit, then don't fuck with me," Ciaran snarled.

"Oh no, you've been protected for centuries. I dare not touch you. But your family is vulnerable. You can tighten the security in your universe to protect them from creatures. But magic has no boundaries. You can only deal with magic by using magic. And I have been informed that magic is the only thing you *don't* have." She smiled again. "I have to leave now. Deal or no deal?"

Ciaran stared into the woman's evil eyes. *You are forcing me to do this*, he thought, and then he said aloud, "All right. It's a deal," he said.

She smiled. "What's the spell?"

Ciaran locked his eyes onto the image of the woman looming over him. "Listen carefully. Here it is. *Psychi abadia sýllipsi.*"

The smile drained from the woman's face, and the whiteness drained from her body. She let out a bloodcurdling scream and exploded into nothingness.

On the ground, Ciaran gasped and awoke in his body. The pain had disappeared. He saw the concerned looks on everyone's faces. He stood up. "Thank you."

"For what? We didn't do anything, Ciaran," Mya said as she gazed at him questioningly.

He glanced around the black and dark landscape. There was a faint mark in the darkened sky where the woman had stood. He wasn't sure if the others could see it, but he was sure they had no idea what he had just done. He had cast the soul catcher spell, one that Iilos, the teacher of the soul traders, had designed for him. She had told him it should only be used in an emergency situation as the cost for using it could be unimaginable.

"What?" Zach said.

"What's what?" Ciaran asked.

"You said let's go back to Camelot. Where the heck is that?"

Ciaran shook his head. He had no idea when and why he had said that. "I meant let's get back to Eudaiz."

CHAPTER 29

Kirra brought some water into the bedroom and checked on Dex. He had been out for quite a while, which left her with some time to search around his house and nose into his business. Her injuries were almost healed, and she looked almost normal now. That proved the medicine he had given her had worked, so she fed him some, too.

After a wild search of his house while he was out, Kirra could sketch a picture of his life—or lives for that matter. Nothing could weird her out after witnessing what had happened in the week since she had run into Zach, Mya, and Leon. Even so, she still didn't like Dex's full name or the fact that he kept grabbing her hands and calling her Elanora in his delirium.

She could figure her way out of here. She was a trained tour guide, after all, and she had a knack for adventure. She didn't think the underworld was any different from other worlds. It had to have entrance and exit point. But she didn't like leaving Dex by himself when he was sick as a dog. No matter what had happened, it appeared he had run into the fire to save Elanora, effectively saving her body as well. If he hadn't done that, she wouldn't have been able to get back into it now. He was a marshal. It had a nice ring to it. And his actions had proven that there were some good aspects to his nature. So she stayed.

On the bed, Dex stirred and opened his eyes. She brought water over to him and sat at the bedside. "My medicine seems to have worked well on you," she said and smiled.

He chuckled and sat up, leaning against the headboard. "There is a side effect, though. It'll turn me into a woman."

She grinned. "I'd love to see that. Now, are you hungry?"

He frowned.

"You don't eat?

He smiled. "No, I'm trying to remember the last time we had a meal together. But yes, I'd like some food. I'm starving."

"All right then." She stood and went to the kitchen where she had seen some dried food earlier when she'd looked around. One of the skills she was proud of was her cooking. She could cook a gourmet meal out of nothing but thin air, but this was quite a decent kitchen.

Before she could finish preparing the meal, there was a loud bang, and the door flew open. She hurried into the living room to hide behind the breached door. Peering through the gap between the door and the frame, she saw a group of ancient soldiers storming into the bedroom. Behind them, an authoritative-looking woman in a long golden dress sauntered in.

Before she entered the bedroom, the soldiers rushed out, reporting something in to the woman in a language Kirra didn't understand. She recognized some of the words Leon and Mya had used and thought these people must be Babylonian.

There were two gigantic guards at the door, and she wasn't sure she would be able to get past them. The golden woman turned around, looking disappointed. She guessed the soldiers had just reported that Dex wasn't in the room.

Kirra grinned to herself. She knew where he was. When she'd searched the place while Dex was passed out, she had stumbled upon Dex's secret compartment in the bed room.

But before she could think about what to do next, she looked up, and her eyes landed right on the face of the golden woman. The woman said something in Babylonian. She didn't understand but thought it was most likely a sarcastic greeting. With a swing of the woman's arm, the door and half of the wall collapsed. Then her arm started out like a steel wire and it was flying toward her. Kirra staggered back but hit the wall. The woman grabbed her neck and pulled her up, leaving Kirra's legs dangling in the air. She then smashed her body down to the floor.

Kirra saw stars, but she scrambled back up to her feet, cursing, and adopted a fighting stance.

The woman looked at her and smirked. She said something else.

"I don't understand a word you're saying."

The woman paused as she realized Kirra was speaking English. Then she smiled and spoke in English as well. "Tell me where your lover is, and I'll let you live."

"I don't know what you're talking about." She copped a hard hit to the face for that remark. "That's enough. You stormed into my house and assaulted me. I'll report you."

The woman approached, "To whom? A marshal?" And then she laughed.

Kirra stepped back. Suddenly, an explosion came from right beneath her feet. She dropped down to the hole, and the next thing she knew, she was in Dex's arms. He put her down and grabbed her hand. "Run," he said.

Dex threw a smoke bomb behind him and took her hand, running along what looked like a dark tunnel. After a while, he stopped.

"You don't think they'll chase us?"

Dex shook his head. "No. It's a narrow tunnel. They don't know where it leads. They won't want to be ambushed."

"Where does it lead?"

He looked at her. "Earth. I'm taking you back to your friends. What's your name?"

"When did you figure out I wasn't Elanora?"

He smiled. She had never seen a smile so sad before. "Elanora doesn't cook." He tilted her chin up and looked into her eyes. "If I was in my cat form, I'd know instantly whose soul was in this body. But in this human form, I can't tell the difference between souls. However, I know personality traits. You're a world away from Elanora."

"I'm Kirra."

"Thank you, Kirra, for not giving me up back there."

"I don't do that to friends—I mean, to anyone."

He chuckled. "You're too good for the underworld."

"I'm not so sure about that. But how will you find Elanora now that she's out of my body?"

He gestured ahead as they kept walking. "Hunting fugitives is my job. The same principle applies to finding missing persons—or missing souls in this case."

"So, you just go around hunting fugitives for the underworld as a freelancer?"

Dex laughed. "You dug around in my files."

She shrugged. "I have to know who I'm dealing with."

"In this world, they call me a rogue. But freelancer will do. And yes, that's what I do. I've done it for a long time. The woman back there is Ishtar, the Goddess of—"

"Ishtar! The one who cheated Mya for thousand years and kept her in debt so she could use her?"

Dex nodded. "Yes. That's the one. She wanted to know which fugitive I'm hunting in her world."

"Apparently you can't tell her. But she's a Goddess. A fugitive she cares about must be somewhat important. What kind of marshal *are* you, hunting fugitives of that caliber?"

Dex looked at her. "You're a smart woman, Kirra." Then he pointed at the dim light at the end of tunnel. "That's Earth."

CHAPTER 30

Leon was walking toward the helicopter with Mya, Ciaran, and Zach. He glanced behind and shuddered at the scene that had just happened when Ciaran and Mya killed hundreds of lost spirits. The giant woman that looked at him with fire in her eyes, he was sure she was a soul trader. And Casey had told him that his soul cannot be traded. So he challenged the woman. But damn, the woman had exploded before he could do anything.

But he was sure Ciaran had somehow killed the soul trader. He didn't have any hopes of getting the information out of Ciaran easily. But he promised himself he would give it a go when he had a chance. He was Zach's successor and Zach was the second councillor. Ciaran was the king of Eudaiz. They ought to teach Leon some useful skills, and that should in crude how to kill a soul trader. Leon was engrossed in his thoughts and almost jumped out of his skin when Casey called him.

"My God!"

"Oh my, goddammit!" he exclaimed.

Everyone turned and looked at him. "I'm talking to someone right now. She is invisible to everyone, including me. So please don't think I'm crazy." He glanced around, having no idea where to look, and said, "Speaking of the devil, Casey, I've been thinking about you along with the whole soul trader ordeal we just encountered. But if you don't mind, can you wait until we get into that big bird and Ciaran gets us out of here before you tell me what you want?"

"I need your help right now, my God!"

"Stop calling me God." Leon smiled and explained to everyone, "She calls me God all the time."

"When did you get to know this...woman?" Zach asked.

"In Sydney. It's a long story. She's a soul trader."

"A what?" everyone chorused.

"Did they just kill a lot of spirits here?" Casey asked.

"Yes, Casey. And they also killed a giant woman I believe is a soul trader. So I don't think they'll like you too much."

"I didn't do anything wrong."

"I'm not saying you did. But we just had a fight right here, and we're tired. Can we get out of here before we talk?"

"I really need your help right now."

"All right, but only if you can make the others hear you so I don't have to repeat everything you say to them. If they agree to help you—"

"Please help me. I'm Casey. Can you hear me?"

"Yes," everyone said at once.

"I'm sorry for my intrusion. I possessed a very important talisman before I become formless like this. Richard, my manager, was going to give the talisman to my son for me. He held it in his hand when he said he loved me. And the talisman branded him."

Zach waved his arms. "Wait a second, lady. We have a life and death situation here, and we need to get out of here as soon as we can. And you want us to go help your lover because he has some kind of a love tattoo?"

"It's not Richard who needs help. It's the talisman. I couldn't find my son. Someone has to take it to where it belongs. It has branded a lover and will lose its power very soon."

"You're not making any sense, Casey. What exactly do you want us to do? And why should we help you?" Ciaran asked, stepping up from behind Zach.

"Oh my god," Casey gasped.

"Stop calling me," Leon growled.

"I think that was just an exclamation, Leon," Zach said.

"Who are you?" Casey asked. "The one in the bloody shirt."

"Ciaran LeBlanc. And for your information, I have just killed a giant soul trader."

"Of course you did. Because you can."

"I don't know what you mean, but I don't really care for an explanation. We're leaving." Ciaran turned to leave.

"You have to get the talisman for me," Casey snarled.

"I don't think that's the tone people use to ask for help. And I second what Ciaran just said," Zach said, turning to follow Ciaran.

"If you are who you say you are, show yourself," Mya said.

The image of Casey Anderson flickered rapidly but stayed about ninety percent transparent. "Due to an accident, I have temporarily lost my form. But this should be enough for a presentation."

Casey locked her gaze on Ciaran for a second then said, "Who would have thought?" She reached her arms out, and as soon as that happened, a fireball flew from Mya toward her.

"You lay a finger on his soul, and I swear to my Goddess, I'll burn you to ashes," Mya snarled.

Casey raised her hands, seeking a truce. "All right, I won't touch his soul. Please hear me out."

Ciaran tapped Mya's shoulder to calm her down and stepped forward. "You have one chance to convince us to help you. Make it count."

The flickering image of Casey looked at Ciaran. She stepped closer. Mya inched forward behind Ciaran. Zach gripped her shoulder to hold her back. Leon could feel the intense energy in the air. He pushed forward.

"Casey, just tell them why they have to get the talisman."

"They won't believe me."

"As I've said, you have one chance," Ciaran said patiently.

Casey looked at Ciaran then back at Leon. "Go on, tell him," Leon said.

Casey nodded. "The talisman is the proof that you were created out of true love."

"Oh, fuck no!" Zach shouted. "Ciaran, let's go."

Ciaran's eyes were as cold as steel. He said nothing, turned around, and walked away.

"What's wrong?" Leon asked and followed Ciaran and Zach. From the corner of his eyes, he saw that Casey was confused and upset. She reached her hands out after Ciaran. "No, Casey," Leon shouted. But it was too late. A second fireball flew from Mya toward Casey. But instead of setting Casey on fire, Mya was thrown several feet away. She hit the ground and rolled .

"No, Mya," Zach shouted and ran toward her. She scrambled up to her feet and threw another fireball. The fire fizzled out, and she was thrown again, this time passing out on the ground.

"Stop that, Casey!" Leon shouted.

"I didn't do anything wrong!" Casey said.

Zach blasted his sound waves at her. Casey cried out.

"Go away, Casey!" Leon shouted.

Zach blasted again.

Casey screamed in pain. The waves bounced back at Zach, and he staggered, blood trickling down his nose.

Ciaran approached Casey. "You forced me to do this," he said.

"Kill me, and you will regret it."

Leon heard Ciaran said something strange. It sounded like a spell. Everything moved too fast for him to react. The next thing he knew, Ciaran's body, like Mya's, was hurled several feet in the air. He shot away as if he were a cannonball and then dropped down through a tree to the ground. He lay there, fifty feet away, totally out.

"What did you do? Did you kill him, Casey?" Leon shouted.

Casey started crying. "I didn't do anything," she said.

"Go away," Leon growled.

"Can I take a look at him?"

"No, if anything happens to them, I will never forgive you. Go away."

Casey nodded a goodbye and vanished.

A short distance away, Zach had helped Mya up. She was still groggy. Leon darted toward Ciaran.

"How is he?" Zach asked.

"I don't know," Leon said. "He's been stabbed by a tree branch. It's just shoulder wound, but he's not breathing."

"I don't know where the fuck his eudqi point is," Zach growled.

"It might be just the shock of the fall," Mya said. She could feel every ounce of muscle in Zach's body trembling. "It might be just a flesh wound. And like you, he'll heal fast. Don't you lose it, Zach. We need you."

Zach said nothing. His eyes were dark, and his lips formed a thin line. Mya knew he did that when he was either unsure or angry. They approached Ciaran and Leon. A small but sharp-looking tree branch protruded from the left side of Ciaran's chest. Mya knew that with the Eudaizian energy in him, the only thing they had to worry about was his eudqi point.

Zach peeled Ciaran's bloody shirt off. "Fuck me," he muttered. The tree had pierced his chest just a couple of inches from a faint round mark that Mya knew by now that was his eudqi point.

"It's a flesh wound, right?" Leon asked.

Zach said nothing.

"Yes, Leon. But it's a serious one," Mya said.

Zach concentrated. "I have to get the branch out. He can't heal himself when it's in there." He grabbed the tree branch and pulled it out in one swift move. Blood spurted from the wound. Ciaran gasped and resumed his breathing.

Zach slid a hand under Ciaran's neck, checking. "A fall at that angle could have broken his neck," he explained.

"When he was out before, his soul led us through the healing area to heal his body. It will do that again," Mya said.

"So it wasn't his mind that brought us here. Are you sure, Mya?" Zach asked.

"More sure than ever. My fireball bounced back at me when I tried to stop Casey from getting Ciaran's soul because she hadn't done anything wrong. That means she's entitled to catch Ciaran's soul. I couldn't hear the spell Ciaran used, but if it was the same one he used to kill the giant soul trader, but this time, it bounced back hard at him, I can only think of one reason— Casey is his soul's creator.

CHAPTER 31

Casey waited a brief moment for Richard to wake. She had just put him out a bit while she ran to Leon for help after failing to contact Dex. She didn't have permission to go to the underworld, but most of the time, Dex was quite responsive whenever she needed him. It was lucky that she had tagged Leon during their brief encounter. He was a minor God, but he didn't know that. The most important thing was that Casey could tell Leon had a kind nature, regardless of what kind of God he was. She couldn't believe the tag had led her to meet Leon again at the soul market and then to meeting one of her great creations—the king's spirit.

It had been such a long time. She didn't think she'd ever see him again. She didn't know why his attempt to attack her had led to his body being harmed so badly. She wanted to protect him. She had done it once. She could certainly do it again.

"Richard, could you do me a favor?"

Richard sat up on the floor and frowned.

"Sorry, you were in shock when the talisman branded you. You were out for a bit."

He nodded and stood up, looking at the burn mark on his palm.

"The mark won't have any residual effects, Richard. It's just a burn. You don't have to worry."

"I'm not worried. What's the favor you want from me?"

"It's regarding the talisman."

"You said you want me to give it to Dex. I can do that."

"Things have gotten a bit more complicated."

"Since when? When I was out?"

"It doesn't matter, Richard. I tried to contact Dex, but he isn't available."

"Give me his address. I'll go get him." Richard paused and then said, "Oh, you're a soul trader, so your son isn't a normal human being. If you can't get him, then neither can I."

"Unfortunately, you're right. You can't go to his house. I need the talisman to be delivered to a safe place. If I had any physical form, I would have done it myself, Richard."

"And I'm guessing the place isn't accessible by ordinary humans."

Casey sighed. "No. And I don't want to put you in danger."

"It's not danger I'm worried about. I don't have any magical abilities. I don't even know how to pray."

"You needn't worry about it. I can send you. But you have to travel across worlds. The travel and the task itself are not dangerous. But because you're a human, if anything happens, and you can't get back to your world—"

"I'll be dead?"

"Yes, clinically dead as a human."

"What does that mean?"

"I have traded your soul once with one of mine. I can't do that again. If anything happens to you again, there' will be nothing I can do."

"What's the location? I mean, spiritual or supernatural or however you want to define it."

"I need the talisman to be delivered to Merlin's cave. Then I need to talk to him to explain a situation."

"All right, at least there's a definite location—a cave with a name. I can do that." Richard picked up the talisman. He wrapped it inside one of Casey's silk scarves and slid it into his pocket.

"I would use the wooden box, but it's quite bulky," he said.

"Thank you."

He paused then looked straight ahead. Casey approached and made herself appear in a flickering image. He looked at her and smiled. "There you are, beautiful."

In her formless body, she could still feel a warm sensation as he spoke those gentle words with his deep voice.

"Tell me what I need to do to get to Merlin's cave. I can't imagine you want me to drive my car across worlds." He chuckled.

She smiled at him. "Just lie down on the bed."

He went over to the bed and sat down. "Can I ask about Merlin's cave? If, as you've said, the trip could be dangerous, I should know where I'm going. And if I might die, I should at least know why."

She sighed. "The talisman is the proof of a king's soul created out of true love. I once took the human form of a queen of a great king. He needed an heir. There was a secret prophecy that he would never have a son, and he believed that prophecy. The king asked for assistance from a wizard. That wizard placed a love spell on me without knowing I am a soul trader. I diverted his spell to the talisman. The love I had for the king was genuine. We didn't need magic to conceive a child together. I have my own power, and I knew the prophecy wasn't true. So I gave birth to the king's son, and he later became one of the great and legendary kings."

Richard nodded. "This sounds awfully familiar," he said.

"The wizard Merlin thought the spell worked on me because I faked the result. When the talisman branded you, it meant his spell is actually working—but on the wrong person. If Merlin's spell didn't work on the queen before, anyone who knew about the prophecy will rule that the king wasn't a legitimate heir."

"Well, it sounds serious. But perhaps more effective if it took place in medieval times..." Richard trailed off then looked at Casey's still flickering image. "Oh my God, this isn't Merlin and King Arthur you're talking about?"

"You know history well, Richard."

"But that's not history. It's a myth. I read about it in a play. We're in the theatrical business, remember? Now you're saying all of that is *real*?"

"As real as can be. One of the live forms I've taken was Igraine, king Uther's wife. I was her. So I know the truth."

Richard looked at his palm then at Casey. "All right. Let's say it's history. That means it has already happened. If they find out now that the spell didn't work before, it's still history. There's nothing they can do, right? The most damage they could do is to change history books—if they can even do that without concrete facts to support it."

"It's not history I'm worried about, Richard. It's the future. Have you heard of the multiverse?"

"No."

"Have you heard of time travel?"

"In the movies."

"Well, I did more than just give birth to an heir. Before Arthur died, I preserved his king's spirit and passed it on to a different family, but I cannot tell you about that. I've lost track of Arthur's heir since then. But because of the king's spirit, the family has become powerful and now holds a great portion of the balance of power in the cosmos. If I were the adversaries of that family, and I figured out this secret, and I could time travel or conjure magic or both, what do you think I would do?"

Richard nodded. "I understand—they'll do everything in their power to make sure that with the family never existed or the power never come to them."

"Now you can feel my pain."

"So you want me to get this talisman to Merlin's cave. And somehow you'll convince Merlin—if he's alive—that although his magic didn't work, the child was legit. But still, what would stop the time travelers or wizard from coming back and changing the course of history?"

"That's why I want Merlin to change history himself. He has to prove the prophecy didn't exist and he didn't perform the magic in the first place."

Richard frowned. "So Merlin is still alive?"

Casey smiled. "No. Unfortunately not. He's a wizard, but he's human. He died a long time ago. If you get the talisman for me, I will be able to travel back in time."

"Y-you can time travel?"

"Not the way you see in movies. But I have my own way of doing so."

"It can't be that easy."

"No, it's not easy at all. Your transport to Merlin's cave is dangerous. And my time travel isn't without costs to myself. If it were easy and free, everyone with a bit of magical power would be traveling back and forth to make a profit for themselves."

"So what does this time travel cost you?"

"You don't need to know that, Richard."

"If you won't' tell me, I'm not going to do it."

"You know enough, Richard. If this information got into the wrong hands, you can't imagine the degree of destruction it might cause."

"You're not God, Casey. You don't have to do this."

"No, I'm not God, but I had the privilege to live many lives over those many thousand years. I have to give something back somehow. I've seen many civilizations. This current time is one of the better ones, and I'd like to help it continue to exist. And I'm talking about more than humans and this Earth. I mean the multiverse. Will you help me, Richard?"

"I have one condition. If I make it back here alive, you promise to be with me for the rest of my natural life no matter what form you're in. I have to have you. I'm sorry if I'm being selfish. But I'm human, and I'd like to make the most of however many years are left in my life...with you."

Casey nodded. "Yes, I promise."

CHAPTER 32

In the helicopter, Mya and Leon were trying to get Ciaran back to the healing zone. He kept vomiting blood. Zach help his head up and cushioned it against a medical bag so he wouldn't choke.

"Let's form a circle here, and you guys will bring us back, right?" Zach asked.

"We'll try, but there's no guarantee. We didn't get there by ourselves," Mya said.

Leon frowned and let his hands flop to his sides.

"Leon, we need to form a circle in order to take Ciaran out of here. What's the matter?" Zach asked.

"It was his soul that led us there because it wanted to heal Ciaran's bodily injuries. Now he's injured because he fought with his soul creator. I guess he's not supposed to catch the soul of this soul creator. So in a case like this, if we channel, will his soul still allow us into the healing zone? What if it wants to punish his body? What if it thinks he deserves to die because he fought his creator?"

Mya looked at Zach. "Leon has a valid point, Zach."

Leon continued. "Why did you object when Casey explained why we should help her with the talisman?"

"That has nothing to do with this," said Zach.

"Everything helps, Zach," Mya said. "If we channel, we need to make sure his soul isn't going to lead us to some dead zone. Casey said the talisman proves Ciaran was created out of true love. What's wrong with that?"

"He wasn't born from true love. He was born from a terrible moral crime against his parents."

"And he told you that?" Leon asked.

"I was unfortunate enough to witness his family story unfold. People he cared for died so he could live. If you make Ciaran go through that again, I swear to you, he'll burn the multiverse down."

"But Casey would have meant the creation of his *soul*, not the conception of himself as a human," Mya said.

Zach shook his head. "But we didn't know about this soul creation when she mentioned it. And it's irrelevant now. If you're sure his soul controls the channel to get to the healing zone, do you think it would work now, now that it knows he struck Casey by mistake?"

Mya looked at Leon. "What do you think?"

"I don't think we have any other option. We have to take our chances."

Mya nodded. They formed a circle and did what they had done before. Zach closed his eyes. He felt the movement of the helicopter and the energy that went through their connected hands. Then the movement stopped. Zach opened his eyes and zeroed in on Ciaran.

Unlike the last time, Ciaran opened his eyes groggily and didn't sit right up to declare he was free from injuries. "Help me up, please," he said.

Leon looked outside the window. Seeing nothing around, he opened the helicopter door.

Zach helped Ciaran sit up and leaned him back against the chair. Ciaran continued, "It was my fault for attacking Casey."

"You didn't know," Mya said.

"She should have given a better explanation," Leon said.

"What's now, Ciaran?" Zach asked.

"I have an extra soul in me, if that makes any sense," Ciaran said.

"Yes, I've seen it," Mya said.

Ciaran nodded. "Her name is Lyla. She's a very young soul trader and probably inexperienced. I think she is healing me just now. The soul Casey created in me is another one, and that one has refused to help because I attacked its creator."

Zach repeated Mya's words. "You didn't know, Ciaran."

"I don't know how it works or how to explain that to a soul." Ciaran smiled weakly. "I don't have a choice of what I can and can't take for my soul. The healing here isn't complete. I have to go back to Eudaiz. I don't have your jar with me now. Sorry, Mya."

"I didn't have it for a thousand years, so why hurry now?" Mya said. "How do we get you back to Eudaiz? We don't even know where we are now."

"Merlin's cave," said a male voice, causing Zach and Leon to draw their weapons. Ciaran wanted to react but figured he was too weak to do so, so he sat still.

At the door of the helicopter, a man appeared and reached his hand in. "I'm Richard Lane. I'm the manager of the Magicz Theatre. I really need to get into this narrow cave, and of course, your helicopter parked right in front of it. I'm just going to sneak around your helicopter to squeeze in. I just wanted to let you know so you wouldn't shoot at me thinking I'm trying to do something to your aircraft."

"Magicz Theatre? You based in Sydney," Zach said.

"Yes, we have been for the last year. But we're about to move on soon."

"So where are we now?" Mya frowned.

"Merlin's cave," Richard said again.

"Are you human?" Leon asked.

Richard withheld a laugh and said, "Last time I checked, yes. If you'll excuse me, I'd like to finish this task quickly and get back to Sydney. That way I'll remain human—and alive—both of which are quite desirable to me." Richard gestured toward the left of the helicopter and was about to leave.

"Who sent you here?" Ciaran asked.

"Excuse me? I mean, no one sent me."

Ciaran growled, more because he didn't have the energy to speak up rather than because he was angry. "You're obviously human because you can't tell we have minor gods in front of you. You can't come here by yourself as an ordinary human. So who sent you?"

"Hey, I don't need to talk to you. I was just trying to be polite," Richard snapped.

Before he could turn around, Zach had snatched his collar. "Whoever sent you here will get you back to Sydney. We're going to have to hitchhike if you don't mind. So I'm afraid we can't let you go inside the cave by yourself because you might disappear after you finish what you're here to do. We'll go in with you. Once you're finished, we'll go with you back to Sydney." Richard shoved Zach away, but Zach wouldn't let go. Zach snarled, "Either we go back with you, or you stay here with us. Your choice."

"All right, all right." Richard pushed Zach hand's off his shirt. "Then let's go."

"Can you walk?" Zach asked.

Ciaran nodded.

Leon and Zach flanked Ciaran's sides, helping him to walk. Mya walked next to Richard to be sure he didn't try to bolt ahead.

"Just for your information, one of my best talents as a minor deity is that I can run like wind. So don't ever think about outrunning me," Mya said. "And Leon can simultaneously kill dozens of leopards and two-headed lizards. You don't want to make him angry. Zach can cleave your skull in half with sound waves. And Ciaran can dig you a grave as big as the Grand Canyon with his mind blade."

Richard stared at Mya briefly and then said, "Just for your information, when I accepted this task, death was number one on the list of risks. I'm not easily scared. But if it makes you feel better, young lady, I am intimidated by the talent profile of your group. Now can we go?"

CHAPTER 33

The cave got darker and more eerie as they went deeper inside. The walls of the cave were black and damp as if it was sweating. Thousands of small blue and green particles glittered, lighting their way. Something hummed a haunting chant as if inviting them to hell. And the group pressed on.

At the end of the cave, a magnificent hundred feet wall opened upward like a dome. The charcoal wall of the cave was plain, and the round surface in front of the wall was empty. It looked like an abandoned temple.

"Okay, Richard, is this where you're supposed to deliver your object? Zach asked.

Richard nodded. He approached the wall and touched it. The wall shuddered. Dirt and mist at least a thousand years old oozed out into the thick air.

"Get back! Something is waking," Mya said.

Leon and Zach pulled Ciaran backward.

"You get back here as well, Mya. It's a dead end. He isn't going to run anywhere," Zach said, nodding at Richard.

Mya nodded and stepped back.

On the wall, something moved. Richard startled and jumped backward. Then he cleared his throat and said, "I have an object to deliver to you. The owner of the object said it contains one of your spells."

"You dare disturb my sleep?" an old man's voice said from the wall. Richard jumped several steps backward then held his ground in the middle of the domed area.

"I don't mean to disturb you. I need to talk to Merlin."

"I am not interested in talking to you. Get out of my cave."

"So you're Merlin. I'd like to let you know that one of your old spells didn't work as you might have thought."

"I conjured thousands of spells during my time. Why do you think one failed spell would concern me?"

"But you only created one spell to create a great king."

The wall shuddered again. "Don't you dare stand here making accusations about my magic. That spell in particular was legendary. Don't you dare say otherwise."

The wall shuddered again, and a thousand years' worth of dirt rained down to the ground. Something on the wall cracked. The shape of an old man's face appeared, and the eyes opened.

Richard yelped and staggered back another few steps. He looked around and saw the group still standing and waiting for him at the other end of the room. Embarrassed, he turned back to the face in the wall.

"I have proof!" He raised his right palm so that it faced the wall. "Your spell branded me."

"You're Casey's lover. The guy with the love tattoo!" Zach said.

Richard turned around. "What?"

"Never mind. Show him. He's waiting," Zach said.

Richard returned to show his palm to the eyes on the wall. The eyes sparked with anger. None of them could see where the mouth was, but they heard humming roars echoing from somewhere. The eyes opened wider now and started scanning the area.

"It's not my fault. I'm just the messenger. Here is your object." He put the talisman on the ground.

"Who sent you?"

"Look, it's not my place to explain this."

"*Who sent you?*"

"Okay...it was Casey Anderson."

"Who is she?"

"That's irrelevant. She will explain to you."

"Who is Casey Anderson? How can she know about my spell?"

"It's not Casey. I mean, it wasn't her in that life. She used to be Igriane..."

At the back of the cave, Zach whispered, "This isn't going to go down well. We should leave."

"Agreed," Leon said.

Mya nodded.

"I can't run," Ciaran said.

Zach and Leon flanked Ciaran's sides again to support him.

Inside the dome, they heard a roar. "She diverted my spell!"

"Shit!" Zach muttered. Sparks and beams of light erupted from the eyes of the wall face, blasting across the room and lighting up the dim cave. The group turned to face the dome to see what was coming at them.

Then the angry roar died out.

Richard had fallen to his knees in the middle of the dome.

"Poor guy," Mya muttered. She raised her voice. "He's just a messenger!"

Richard stood up and brushed the dirt off his hands and knees. "I'm okay. Thanks for your concern. I came here prepared for the worst. Only because Casey said this might have an impact on the balance of power in the multiverse. I don't know what the multiverse means, but it seems like a lot of people and creatures could die. I'm only a man, but if I can help fix it, I should."

"Come here. Let me see you," Merlin said.

"I've shown you the talisman and the mark on my hand. What else do you want to see?" asked Richard.

"Not you. Arthur. Let me see you. Now it's proven that you're not my creation. But still, I'd like to see you."

The eyes blinked, waiting.

Silence.

Ciaran stood, leaning against the cave wall. "None of us here is Arthur. Merlin, I understand your magic is important to the relationship between Uther and Igraine. Everyone knows this story from history. But it's a myth. For some reason, Casey, or Igraine, has mistaken me as Arthur before. But my name is Ciaran LeBlanc. And my family has nothing to do with the Pendragons."

Richard stared at Ciaran. "So it was you..."

"He just explained that it wasn't him. Is my English so poor that I misunderstood that?" Leon asked.

Richard approached Ciaran and the group. "Are you from the multiverse? Are you someone of importance?" he asked Ciaran.

Zach snarled, "We don't have any idea where we are. And at the moment, you're arguing with a

THE GOOD DEITY 2 – ALMOST SURE

wall. Even if we were, do you think we would admit to anyone that we're holding significant power over *anything*?"

"Let me see you, Arthur!" Merlin said again.

Richard said, "Casey said she took the king's spirit before he died and placed it in another family. And that family is now holding a significant balancing power in the multiverse. You've got to be the one, Ciaran."

Ciaran's eyes were as cold as steel. "We're leaving."

"I can heal you, Arthur. You're injured. You won't make it back to wherever you came from," Merlin said.

"I don't have King Arthur's spirit," Ciaran told the wall. His anger drew energy from him, and he grabbed at a bit of stone on the uneven cave wall to keep his body standing upright.

"If you have such great power, you wouldn't be stuck in a wall, would you? How can we know that you can do what you claim?" Zach said.

"I've made a mistake. That's why I'm imprisoned here. But my magic still works."

"Mya, is there a way to guarantee he only heals my body and doesn't affect my mind or soul or anything else? I don't care much for being possessed or controlled," Ciaran asked.

"If you walk out of this cave, I'll never help you," Merlin said.

Mya looked at Ciaran. He didn't look like he could make it out of the cave anyway. "There's no guarantee, Ciaran. I'll do my best to prevent it from happening. You just have to trust me."

"You learned that lesson during your coronation, Ciaran. Sometimes you have to trust people. I trust her with my life," Zach said.

Ciaran nodded, giving Mya the go-ahead signal.

"Stay here, all of you," Mya said and strode toward the center of the dome. She pulled out her deity badge and showed it to Merlin. "My name is Mya Portman, and I am a minor deity. I' have been in charge of thousands of souls over more than a thousand years. I work under the protection of Ishtar, the Goddess of Love and War. If you go against me or cause myself or my subjects any harm, you will declare war with my Goddess. You're a smart man, Merlin. You should know the consequences of making my Goddess angry."

Merlin blinked. "Yes, Ishtar has a reputation. I understand."

Mya nodded. "Now, you are going to heal the body of Ciaran LeBlanc from injuries, and your healing is limited to that body in this time only. You are not to use your magic or power to influence any spiritual part, including his mind, his souls, and the king's spirit. Violating that means you will declare war to the eternity with Ishtar, the Goddess of War and Love. Am I understood?"

"Wow, she turns me on when she adopts that authoritative tone," Zach said.

One of Merlin's eyebrows lifted. "Since when is the king's spirit of Arthur your subject?"

Ciaran said, "I appoint Mya Portman as the guardian of all spiritual matter carried by my body. The position is effective immediately and will be valid as long as she shall live and in all territories of the multiverse, including all spiritual and mind dimensions."

Zach grinned. Mya smiled at Merlin until he lowered his lifted eyebrow. "Can we proceed?" Mya asked.

"All right," Merlin said.

"Let's go," Zach said. Zach and Leon helped him walk to the middle of the domed area. The eyes shone, scanning left and right.

"Is he a lighthouse?" Zach muttered. "If we leave you here, can you stand for a few seconds?" Zach asked.

"Yes. Thank you. Just leave me here."

The light from the wall scanned up and down and covered everyone in the dome. "It's itchy...stop that," Leon grumbled and brushed at his neck.

Zach and Leon left Ciaran and moved back to the tunnel wing.

"Remember what was said, Merlin," Mya warned as she left the area.

The light exploded in the dome area. Ciaran's body was spun around, and it swung within the funnel of light. Millions of shiny particles floated around.

After a while, the spinning slowed. The light dimmed, and Ciaran was placed gently on the ground. When the light had completely vanished, Ciaran opened his eyes and stood up. He turned toward the group. His eyes sparked with energy, and his king's aura had returned. He smiled at them then turned to Merlin.

"Thank you. If there's anything I can do for you, please let me know."

"Indeed, there is a favor I need from you. I need you to leave the son of my enemy here with me. I have to take him."

"Who is that?" Ciaran asked.

Rolls of dust fumed out from the wall, making them all cough. Leon grabbed his throat and fell to the ground, gasping.

"Him!" Merlin said.

"We come as a group. We'll leave as a group. He's one of my people."

"I will take him," Merlin growled and hummed a chanting spell. Leon's eyes rolled back. His body was pulled onto the floor and out to the dome area then flipped in the air. Magical light beams blasted onto his back and tore off his shirt. He screamed in pain as the skin in the middle of his back was scraped off, revealing a tattoo of a moon.

Mya darted over to Leon. Ciaran and Mya dragged him into the tunnel.

"Get him out of here!" Mya shouted.

Zach and Richard carried Leon, charging along the tunnel. Ciaran held Mya back. Standing in the tunnel, be blasted his mind blade and the wall. Merlin roared. Ciaran blasted again. Mya hurled her fireballs at the wall.

"Why do you have to do this, Merlin?" Mya asked.

"I have to kill him. His mother imprisoned me." Merlin blew out more dust.

"That's not his fault. If you keep doing this, I'll kill you for real, Merlin!" Ciaran said.

Merlin kept roaring and blowing out dust.

"This dust is doing nothing to us, but he is casting a spell on Leon," Mya said.

Ciaran glanced back at the angry eyes on the wall. "You asked for this." He turned and said, "Let's go." They charged out of the mouth of the cave. Mya could see Zach's eyes were bloodshot. Leon was lying on the ground.

"Oh, no." She rushed toward Leon.

Ciaran turned to the cave. Inside the tunnel, more dust was coming out. He concentrated and blasted his gigantic mind blade, digging up the entire hillside. The helicopter dropped into the hole his blade made. Everything exploded, from the mouth of the cave to the dome inside.

He turned around and ran toward the group.

"Casey is taking you back, right?" Mya asked.

Richard nodded.

"Form a circle!" she shouted. Ciaran dove at the group and grabbed for their hands, closing the circle. An explosion cracked the ground, and the crack ran toward them. They vanished, channeling out of the dimension just before the explosion reached their position.

CHAPTER 34

Elanora walked out to the open field in the Australia outback. She squinted in the bright sunlight that reflected on the humid air. She frowned at the feel of the heat on her fragile skin. Well, not exactly her skin, but Kirra's skin. She didn't mind it. What bothered her was that she didn't understand why she was standing in the middle of an open field.

She looked back and saw the gateway between worlds closing and the shadow of Dex standing at the closing door. She wanted to call to him but stopped herself from doing so. She had many questions that needed answers, but she was on a mission. So she turned around and darted toward the stretch of woodland, running toward her secret place.

The place was the same—a small cottage, tucked away between two giant red rocks. The cottage was protected by a spell from a wizard she trusted. No ordinary eyes could see it. She pushed the door open and entered.

The living room looked the same, plain but efficient. The cottage had belonged to her mother, a condemned leopard shapeshifter. She touched the floral tablecloths her mother had made—apart from having her, the handmade table cloths were the only object her mother had left behind in this world that had some meaning, some significance. *Am I a significant individual at all?* she wondered. Elanora frowned. She wasn't sure.

Her mother's life had been dull. But that was because she had chosen to live a quiet life so that Elanora could gain traction in the clan and become their leader as her father had always wanted. Her mother had borne him a child and had never asked for anything in return.

Her father was a high-ranked lynx, and his wife had not given him a child before her death. He refused to remarry but agreed to accept a mate so that he could have an heir. That was how she was created. She threw a table into the corner of the house. She hated the lynx mating rituals. She hated the life her mother had had and the sacrifice she had made.

She had to go to the gateway and find her father. She opened her mother's secret compartment. Taking the talisman, a token of her love to her father, she tucked it into her pocket and left the house.

As soon as she stepped out of the house, her head perked up. She sensed the opening of the gateway. She whirled around, sniffing at the air. She was sure of it. It was opening right now. She could crash the gate if she got there in time. There was no need for hunting down the wrist units of those Eudaizians.

She charged down the road, heading in the direction of the opening.

***

Inside the tunnel, Dex turned and glanced down the corridor with caution. Ishtar didn't seem to be in chase. She wasn't stupid. Dex knew for sure Ishtar was a master at war games, and one of the rules was to never follow subjects into unknown dark spaces.

The compass in his pocket buzzed.

He took it out. It must have been buzzing for a while, but with the degree of activities going on, he hadn't heard it. It wasn't a compass for direction. Rather, it navigated the energy channel across worlds. Given the nature of his work, the device was handy. It was also an effective tool for him to keep tags on his mother.

His heart skipped a beat when he saw it. His mother was in danger.

Her cursed and headed back toward the gate to Earth, the same gate he had just seen Kirra through.

CHAPTER 35

The group landed at the outskirts of Wagga Wagga. From the hillside, they could see the town in the distance. Leon could see his body on the ground. Ciaran took his pulse and shook his head. Mya cried.

"Oh, no. I'm dead." He hated to see Mya cry. Leon stepped back to gain some momentum, then he ran and jumped onto his body. He bounced back out, rolling on the ground. He stood up and cursed. Then he saw Zach's eyes. They were blood shot and angrily searching the area like a hungry tiger.

Richard looked around, unsure of what to do. "Casey!" he called out.

This was so unfair, Leon thought. He didn't even have the chance to fight for his life. He was angry. He jumped into his body again and bounced back out. Then he saw Casey, rushing at Richard. She was concentrating on making her image appear so that Richard could see her.

"I didn't know you brought friends back with you, Richard. It was heavier than I thought, so I had to land you here, not in Sydney. Plus, there was some energy suction in this area..." Casey's voice trailed off when she saw Leon on the ground. "Oh my God..." She rushed toward Leon's body. "I can't trade his soul. What happened?"

"Bastard has my eudqi inside his body. He can't die that easily," Zach muttered as he blasted sound waves at Leon.

"Ouch," Leon grunted and grabbed at his ears. He felt a suction pulling him into his body. *This might work*, he thought. There *was* a way to get back into his body.

Zach blasted again. This time, the suction was stronger. Leon stopped resisting and flew back into his body. As soon as he did so, he had no vantage point from the outside. His world went blank.

"It worked! He's moving," Mya said.

Ciaran walked around, patrolling the area where Zach was blasting energy. Zach stopped and looked at Ciaran. "Keep doing that. It seems to work, Zach," Ciaran said.

"What are you looking for?" Richard asked. "Anything I can do to help?"

"He's blasting out energy. Sound waves. Creatures with a vested interest in our movement will be able to track us," Ciaran said.

"Should we call the cops?" Richard said.

Ciaran glanced around the rolling hillside. "How?"

"Use my cell phone. The signal might be weak. But it's something."

"You've got a cell phone? Why didn't you say so earlier?" Ciaran said, reaching his hand out to borrow the phone.

"You didn't ask. And you can't call a wizard or a god using my phone!"

"No, Ciaran. We were trapped when I called the number you gave me," Zach said.

On the ground, Leon's eyes fluttered and opened, but then his eyes rolled back again.

"No, please stay, Leon," Mya cried.

"Keep him in," Casey said.

"Then what?" Zach asked. "You're a soul trader. Can't you do something?"

"I can't trade his soul. He's a minor god."

"Intruder!" Ciaran shouted and blasted a small mind blade to the middle of the hill. Elanora in Kirra's form jumped out from a small bush. "Gateway," she said and darted at Zach. Ciaran grabbed her from behind. Mya stood up, hands curling into fists.

Held by Ciaran, Elanora wriggled and kicked her legs. "Gateway...I've got to get to the gateway." She slid out of Ciaran's grip and ran toward Zach. Ciaran was about to blast his blade at her, and that would cut her in half.

"No, let her run free. I'll trade her!" Casey shouted.

"You said you can't trade his soul. So what's the cost, Casey?" Richard asked.

"He's a minor God, and he gave my son a pardon. I have to save him at all costs." Casey stood up. Elanora still ran toward Zach. Out of thin air, a gateway flashed open, and Dex jumped out. He snatched Elanora in midair, whirling around so they could gain their footings. When they stood, Elanora growled, "Let go of me. I have to get to the gateway." She pointed at Zach.

Dex looked into her eyes. "It's you. You're back."

"Of course it's me. Who do you think I am? Let go of my hand!"

"Let her go, Dex," Casey said.

"Mother, don't do this. Thousands of years' worth of work. I can't let you finish like this."

"I'm tired, Dex."

"The minor god is falling right into your lap, Mother. His blood will dissolve the curse. Take it, Mother."

"You think I'll let that happen?" Mya said, and a ball of fire flew at Dex and Elanora.

Dex ducked aside, pulling Elanora down with him. Before he could do anything further, Ciaran snatched him away. Zach took the opportunity to charge at Dex. Ciaran and Zach pulled Dex away. Elanora stood and snarled.

Casey raised her arms and chanted her spells.

Thunder rumbled across the sky, and lightning sparked.

Elanora let out a bloodcurdling scream. The soul was sucked out of her body. It floated in the light and exploded.

On the ground, Leon gasped and opened his eyes. Mya rushed toward him.

Zach darted toward Kirra's body, which lay on the ground.

Casey slumped and fell into Richard's arms. Her body had become solid flesh and blood, and it was aging by the second.

Dex kicked Ciaran away and crawled toward Casey. He snatched Casey from Richard and held her body in his arms as she rapidly faded away. Tears rolled down his face. "I'm sorry. I know you loved that woman, Dex," Casey said.

"She chose her path. You didn't choose yours. Mother, please don't leave me."

"I have lived many lives. I have died many times, Dex. You are the best thing that ever happened to me. Stay alive. Be a good marshal."

Dex roared, a haunting roar more animal than human. He placed Casey gently down on the ground. The grief poured out of him. He couldn't control it. His hands turned into paws, and he shifted into his black cat form.

He lowered his head and walked away.

"You're a good marshal. Don't hold this against anyone, Dex," Casey called after him.

Kirra had sat up on the ground. She left Zach's arms to stop Dex. He looked at her with grieving cat eyes. She used her thumb to wipe a tear from a corner of his eye.

"Hello, marshal. Take me with you," she said.

Dex hunched down, and Kirra hopped onto his enormous, muscular back. In the blink of an eye, Dex jumped into his gateway with Kirra atop him, and they both vanished.

CHAPTER 36

Mya smiled at Leon, who had regained some movement on the ground. "Hey, welcome back, minor God."

"Am I being promoted?"

"Yes. By me." She grinned.

"He's still under me. He's my successor," Zach said. He pulled at Leon's hand to help him sit up. Leon glanced around.

"My back hurts." He winced.

"Oh, that's a beautiful little tattoo." Mya grinned.

"Did Merlin brand me?"

"No, I think whatever it is, it was already there. He scraped off your skin to prove you're some kind of important minor god."

"Minor god. That's what Casey has been saying. What happened? I remember seeing Casey. Where is she?"

Richard approached. "She's gone."

Leon stood up. "Gone? Where? Shouldn't you be with her?"

Zach looked at Mya then back at Leon. Mya knew he was going to tell Leon. But she'd rather it came from her. So she cut in. "She traded for your soul although she isn't allowed to do so. As a result, she's gone."

Leon frowned. "But as a soul trader, she's immortal."

"Every person and creature dies, Leon. She has lived for a long time. She knew trading your soul was a serious offense to her God, whoever that might be, and she knew it would be the end of her. But she made her decision. You're not the saddest one here. So please don't make a fuss."

Leon inhaled then exhaled and raised his hands. "No fuss. I'm good." He turned to Richard. "Are you okay? I'm so sorry, Richard."

"I think I'm doing better than you are." Richard patted Leon's shoulder. "It's okay, son. Death is natural." Then he glanced around and saw the look on everyone's faces. "I know you're supernatural creatures. But you all look as if you're barely older than my daughter. So let me say this—I'm sad that Casey is gone, but what Casey and I had together will never go away. At least for me, in this lifetime." He raised his palm with the mark. "I am a happy man. And I will die a happy man. This doesn't happen to everyone. I consider myself lucky. If you have the chance to love someone, treasure every moment."

Mya nodded, deciding not to tell Leon about Dex and Kirra. At least for now.

"I've got a signal," Ciaran said and gave the cell phone back to Richard.

"I hope you didn't call the ones who wanted to turn us in to corpses," Zach said.

"I have no intention of dying today," Ciaran said. "I dropped the jar at the Daimon Gate on the way to Babylon—just in case things went awry. I messaged Madeline the location. It appears she received the message. Our commanders have been sent to retrieve the jar and are delivering it now."

"How did you contact them without your wrist unit?" Zach asked.

"Triangulation. The technology is in beta mode. It's unstable. But we're lucky enough that our head of intelligence anticipated this and has been waiting for the signal."

"Jake? I thought you said he's inexperienced."

"He is. But being young has its advantages. He's certainly tenacious."

Zach shrugged. "Tenacity is what we need now. Get us the hell out of here. Any chance you can message your Goddess, Mya? Or do *we* have to deliver the jar to the court?" Zach asked.

"I can message her," Mya said and closed her eyes, concentrating on her deity mode.

"Richard, you might want to stay out of sight. Behind that tree." Ciaran pointed at a tree in the distance. Richard nodded and strode away.

The air thickened, and a wedge of light shone on the grass. For the people in the distant town, it would look like a rainbow. But up close, it was a teleport. The round circle of light scanned the grass, and two wrist units and a jar appeared.

Then the light changed shades, from a darker blue to a lighter blue and then to white. As it faded in color, it moved away from the objects.

"It turned from teleport into holocast mode," Zach explained to Mya. "Teleport is when people and objects can come in and out and be in presence. Holocast is just a holographic telephone."

"Got it." Mya grinned and looked at the little golden jar sitting on the grass. It seemed to be smiling at her. Her thousand years' worth of debts to the Goddess were about to be paid off. She would be free.

Mya approached the jar and picked it up. Zach stood next to her, rubbing his hand on the small of her back. Then he squeezed her hand slightly. She looked up at him and could see his soft green eyes twinkle. He had anticipated this moment as much as she had. She smiled at him. She wanted to kiss him but thought it would rather be inappropriate, so she pushed the thought away.

In the ring of the holocast, the image of a young man, as beautiful as an angel with blue eyes and sandy hair, looked at Ciaran. "Thank you, Jake," Ciaran said and picked up the two wrist units. He gave one to Zach and put one on his wrist.

"I have commanders on another line, ready at the teleport gate, just in case you need them," Jake said.

Ciaran signaled him to wait. He approached Zach and Mya. "How are we doing?" he asked.

"We're all set. The Goddess is coming to us," Mya said.

Zach tapped his wrist unit. "Jake is brilliant. You should give him a raise."

"He's at the top of his rank. And he's very young. So don't say it to him, or he'll get cocky," Ciaran said.

"All right, I'll tell him this wrist unit is horrible, and I don't like the way he talks," Zach joked.

"Sciphil Two, your microphone is on," Jake's voice came out of Zach's unit. Ciaran rolled his eyes and turned his unit on.

"Jake, commanders on standby for precaution only," Ciaran said.

"Yes, sir."

Jake's image faded away.

In the distance, a gong echoed in the air.

"The Goddess comes," Mya said.

Fifty feet from them, Ishtar appeared with twenty warriors flanking her sides. Mya frowned.

Does she need that many just to accept the jar she was going to give the Goddess anyway? She felt Zach squeeze her hand gently, signaling her not to move.

Ishtar approached, leaving her men behind. "Well, what have we here?" she said in English, locking her eyes on Ciaran.

Ciaran stepped forward and nodded a greeting, "Ishtar, I apologize in advance that I do not know the court etiquette."

"Normally, people fall to the ground and kiss my feet."

Ciaran smiled. He was more than six foot three and towered over the Goddess. "I'm afraid that is not our custom. And I'm very clumsy at kneeling, so I'll be standing instead. In that case, you might have to look up. Furthermore, I don't imagine our conversation will be extensive. You have an agreement with Mya. We are here to fulfill the agreement, and after that, she'll be free from the court."

Ishtar smiled and traced her golden nail down Ciaran's abdomen, who had been walking around shirtless since Merlin's encounter. "Indeed." She turned toward Mya and reached her hand out. "Give me the jar, and you will be free."

Mya inched forward, but Zach pulled her back. "Wait, Ciaran has a plan."

Ciaran stepped away from Ishtar and said, "We have the jar here." He gestured toward Mya. Mya raised the jar so the Goddess could see. Ciaran continued, "We will place the jar on the ground with our protective shield around it. Once we have safely teleported away from this location, then we will lift the shield, and you will be able to retrieve the jar."

"What does that mean? Are you playing tricks on me?"

"No, Ishtar. You've seen the jar. It's a precaution on our part to ensure all of us get back to Eudaiz safely."

"Mya is not yours!" she snarled.

"No one can own her, Ishtar, including you. After we deliver the jar, she is free to go wherever she wants. And I think she might choose to go with my second councillor. In such case, she will be Eudaizian. She will be my people."

"How dare you—"

"I just want to fulfill this agreement in peace."

"Then give me the jar!" A low roar hovered somewhere in the air. Mya knew it was Ishtar's temper. She inched forward, but Zach pulled her back.

"Let's get this over and done with," Ciaran said and walked away from Ishtar. She moved toward her warrior. Then she suddenly turned around and swung her arm at Ciaran.

Mya balled her fists, but Zach stood still and smiled.

The lightning strike from Ishtar hit an invisible wall and shattered into millions of light particles. She staggered back a few steps and growled.

Ciaran raised a hand to signal, and a flash of light cast out, ringing a glowing line around Zach, Mya, and Leon. Ishtar struck at them once more, and her strike shattered again.

Ciaran smiled. "You disappoint me, Ishtar. I thought you were better."

"I am," she roared and raised her arms.

CHAPTER 37

"Give me the jar! I want the jar!" Ishtar roared.

"I said you will have it. But now that you have completely destroyed our confidence that you will fulfill your promises, we will have to deliver it via the shield," Ciaran said and signaled Zach, Mya, and Leon to walk toward him so that they could all teleport away.

"Leon cannot leave!" Ishtar shouted.

"Oh, so that's what it is. You want him *and* the jar. Well, aren't you greedy? Given that he isn't part of the deal, you have to cheat," Zach said.

"Why do you want me, my Goddess? You can easily appoint someone else to be the head of the temple guard," Leon said.

Ishtar prowled around outside the protective shield. Her face grew redder by the second, so much that her temper seeped out through the layers of makeup on her face to become visible on the surface. She wagged a finger with a perfectly polished golden nail at him. "I should have known when the servant picked you up in that little basket that you were not an ordinary baby. I should have known! I should have killed you at that Well of the Death."

"Well, you should have. But it's too late now, Ishtar. Leon has accepted the successor position of Sciphil Two, Zach Flynn. I believe you have a record of this. So he's my people now." Ciaran smiled.

"He's mine!" Ishtar struck the wall of the teleport again but couldn't break through. She roared. "Ciaran LeBlanc, you think you can protect your people in the multiverse? You think *you* are powerful? How about this?"

She stretched out, and her arm grew like a giant steel python. She swung it in the direction of a tree in the distance. The tree and the surrounding area exploded. Richard's body was flung into the air. She grabbed him like a rag doll and pulled him toward where they were standing.

"No, please don't kill him my Goddess," Mya cried out and ran outside the protective shield, but Zach pulled her back. Ciaran signaled. Another teleport beam appeared, from which marched out a group of stealthy Eudaizian commanders.

Ishtar's warriors raised their weapons.

"Humans pray to you, Goddess. You're supposed to protect them. He's an innocent soul!" Mya cried out.

"Do you think I care about pathetic human lives? You want to be a god, Leon? Will you protect these humans if they pray to you? If you want to protect them, then step outside that silly light of yours and face me."

Leon approached the light wall. Ciaran pushed him back inside the protective shield. "Casey died to save you. Try not to waste her sacrifice," Ciaran growled, then signaled his commanders again. They charged. Ishtar warriors roared and advanced. Ciaran's commanders had the most advanced guns in Eudaiz, Ishtar's warriors didn't seem to die. They dropped down when they were fired upon but then stood back up and kept moving forward.

Ishtar smirked. "In a bet between technology and magic, I always put my money on magic, Ciaran. From what I'm told, magic is your weakness. Now let that boy come out, or I'll kill your commanders and this gentleman here."

Mya's hand curled into a ball. Zach saw it and said, "You can't hurl your fire from inside, Mya. You'll burn us.

"So we stay in here like cowards?" she asked.

Ciaran approached the light wall. "This is your last opportunity to call the warriors away and let Richard go. I'll leave the jar for you. That's the agreement you have with Mya. You're a Goddess. Honor your word."

"I don't have to honor my word to anyone. They betrayed me. Someone has to pay." Her steel arm still dangled Richard in the air.

"It isn't his fault that someone betrayed you," Ciaran said.

"What I don't have, nobody can. He has a love spell mark branded on his palm. I don't like it. I don't like him."

"You're not capable of loving anyone or anything. You'll die old and lonely, bitch!" Richard said.

Ishtar roared and ripped Richard's body into hundreds of pieces.

CHAPTER 38

Mya cried out and tried to charge outside, but Zach held her back despite her protests. Ciaran pushed Leon inside again and approached the wall. "You asked for it, Ishtar." He looked at his unit and said, "Jake, do it."

Outside, a funnel suddenly appeared like the nose of a giant vacuum cleaner. All the warriors and the commanders were sucked up and out. Ishtar jumped aside, fell, and scrambled to her feet again. The funnel vanished.

"You sacrificed your commanders. You're no different than I am, Ciaran." Ishtar stood by herself.

"I didn't sacrifice them. They're alive and will be taken out at the other end. There's no guarantee about your warriors, though. This is a Xiilok service. I'm reluctant to use them unless it's absolutely necessary."

"You use Xiilok fighters? You're as evil as I am!" Ishtar screamed.

"You insult me with that comparison. If you're any good as a leader, you should know there are different kinds of Xiilok fighters. I used the good ones." He turned toward Mya. "Leave the jar on the ground for her. We're leaving, Mya."

Mya nodded and put the jar on the ground.

"No!" Ishtar roared. "That bitch had what I didn't. Not only I will kill her, I'll kill generations of her offspring." Her eyes turned red, and she started to chant a curse.

Leon grabbed his chest and heaved. Then he ran out, pulled his knife, and shoved it right through Ishtar's heart.

Ishtar roared in pain.

"I don't know my mother. But no one is going to call her names." He pulled the knife out and stabbed again before Ishtar grabbed Leon and threw him several feet away.

Mya raced toward Ishtar. She dangled the jar in front of her. "Leon or this jar. You can only have one."

"Don't you dare!"

"You don't want to try me."

Zach and Ciaran stepped out of the protective shield. Zach blasted a sound wave at Ishtar. It bounced back at him, pushing him several steps backward. Ishtar smirked. She crooked her finger and waved, and Zach was drawn toward her.

Ciaran shot at Ishtar, immediately realizing the gun wouldn't work on her. He threw a knife at her. It curved back, slashing at his arm.

Ishtar squeezed her fists. Leon heaved and grabbed at his chest again.

"We can't kill her. Get back behind the shield," Ciaran said.

"She'll curse Leon to death. Nothing is going to stop her curse," Mya said and raised the jar again. "I'll destroy it, Ishtar."

Ciaran's wrist unit beeped. He looked at it and said, "Don't worry, Mya. The jar is not to be delivered to Ishtar. I've just received information that the jar is not the potion that raised the dead as she claimed but rather the poison she used to kill the prince of Xiilok. She just wanted the jar so she could destroy the evidence."

"No, I didn't kill him!" Ishtar roared.

Ishtar charged at Mya for the jar. Mya withdrew.

Ciaran said, "For your information, when I left the jar at the Daimon Gate for safekeeping, I sent a sample away for testing. Since we had gone through such trouble to retrieve the jar, I needed to know what was in it. Well, the results came back—it was a potion with your signature toxic compound in it. And that toxin matches the one used to poison the prince of Xiilok."

"That wasn't for him!"

"So it really was poison!" Ciaran smiled.

"I make poison for sport. Many wizards and shamans make toxins. There's nothing wrong with it."

"No, not until the toxin was used for murder," Zach said.

"It wasn't me!" she shouted.

"Oh, so the prince was poisoned by your toxin but not by you?" Leon asked.

Ishtar growled. "It's none of your business."

Mya said, "But it's *my* business because you kept me in debt and made me retrieve a potion that could raise the dead. Now it turns out the jar is evidence of a murder. So you've breached the contract, and I'm off the hook."

"I don't care anymore." Ishtar turned around and was about to leave. Ciaran pressed a series of buttons on his wrist unit.

"You can't leave!" Mya shouted. "You made the poison, but your lover Nunnaki poisoned the prince. That's why he stole the jar from you. That's makes you an accessory to murder."

Ciaran's unit beeped. He glanced at it and tapped a button. Then Zach's unit beeped.

Ciaran said, "The record shows you were engaged to someone in the underworld." The timeline matches up with the incident when Mya let Nunnaki run and, as a result, she owed you a never-to-be-paid-off debt. That means you committed adultery."

"Adultery is the most heinous sin one could commit at the court," Leon said. "I'd take the murder charge if I were you."

"Don't you dare accuse me of anything." The Goddess swung her arm up, but Leon pointed at her, halting her movement.

"I owe you nothing, Ishtar. I resign from the position at your court. And because I am a minor god, if you strike me, it will an unprovoked attack at your own kind." Leon grinned. "You don't want to add that to the crimes of accessory to murder and adultery."

Zach said, "But wait...we have more." He read from his unit. "You were engaged to the prince of Xiilok before he died. There was an uprising, and the prince was about to be declared illegitimate to the throne. Damn, you must have been disappointed and wanted out of the poor deal. So you got engaged to someone else in the underworld. That *double* adultery."

"It's not an adultery if my partner died before I became involved in the next relationship. Do you need to read your textbooks again?"

Ciaran smiled. "You got Nunnaki to kill the prince so you could get out of the engagement. You might have had to promise him something so that he would do that for you."

"Love, she took him as lover," Mya said in disdain.

Ciaran shrugged. "You then became engaged to someone else in the underworld while dating

Nunnaki. That's adultery. Well, unless the person in the underworld died, too,"

"He did!" The words came out before Ishtar could stop them.

Ciaran smiled. "And you know that for sure because you had him killed in a timely manner. At this stage, just between you and me, I think you'd better pick either murder or adultery, whichever one is less severe."

"And in which court of law am I being accused? The Eudaizian? Eudaiz is overrated, Ciaran. Yes, I did it. I love for benefits and kill for sport. So what? What will you do to me? Oh, let me ask that differently—what *can* you do to hurt me? All four of you are standing there at my mercy!" She raised an eyebrow in challenge.

Ciaran winked. "It's tough, isn't it? Here's a bit of advice from me. Between technology and magic, I'd put my money on technology. Have you ever heard of triangulation technology? Probably not, but it's simple. What you have just said is being reflected to multiple dimensions—to the people in Xiilok, to the underworld, and to whomever has authority over you. The trial is being broadcast live to them. My apologies to some panels for the multiversal time differences.

But the short version is...you have just plead guilty in front of your authority."

Ishtar whirled around and around. "Who? What? Where?"

"Come out, Jake," Ciaran said.

The image of Jake appeared, hovering in the air. "This is my head of intelligence. He just helped organize the conference call. Don't shoot the messenger, Ishtar."

Ishtar roared in anger and charged away.

But before she could go anywhere, a gateway opened. Dex and two other marshals jumped out. Dex grabbed Ishtar and snapped a talisman on her shoulder, immobilizing her immediately.

"Ishtar, we are taking you to the underworld for your adultery, murder, and plotting against the underworld authority. To answer the question you asked me when you allegedly beat me up in my own home, the fugitive I was hunting was the crook who ran errands for you when you committed these crimes. We just got him."

As Dex dragged Ishtar away, they heard her voice echoing back. "I was born when you were merely dust. Do you think I'll go down like this? If you love someone, treasure it. Live like there's no tomorrow. Because I'll be back, and I will take it all away from you. What I can't have, nobody will!"

Once they gateway to the underworld closed, a shiny plaque appeared on the ground. Mya picked it up. It stated that she was being summoned to the court of the underworld as a witness for Ishtar's trial.

"Do you have to go?" Zach asked.

"Yes, or it will be as bad as committing the crime itself," Leon said.

"I'll be okay, Zach," Mya said.

"We'll go back to Eudaiz first. I'll get you ready, and we'll go," Ciaran said.

"We?" Mya asked.

"It depends on the trial. If it has significant dealings with Xiilok, I'll have to go with you," Ciaran said.

"Why?" Leon asked.

Zach said, "Xiilok was the last stop of Hoyt Flanagan, our number one enemy and fugitive. Ciaran kicked his ass during the coronation, so he'll spend every waking moment plotting against us. We want to destroy any possible leads that might give Hoyt a chance."

Ciaran continued, "Plus, I used Xiilok rebels for the stunt with the giant suction I just pulled. I think they had something to do with the prince's death as well. I think the men who ambushed me in Babylon are paid by another camp of rebels. So I have some things to sort out."

Leon rolled his eyes. "Why does this have to be so complicated? Can I not be a minor god?"

Mya shook her head and smiled.

CHAPTER 39

The holocast reappeared, and the image of Jake hovered in the air. "Well done, Jake. Thank you," Ciaran said.

Mya looked at Zach and Ciaran discussing their next steps and could see more than an official relationship between them—she saw brotherhood. Whatever her future might be with Zach in Eudaiz, she was sure she would have a happy life with a man who treasured her. She would be surrounded by good people like Ciaran and his friends and his family. For more than a thousand years, there had been many times when she'd lost faith in gods and humanity. But now, in the multiverse, she believed in good karma all over again.

Leon stood by himself, admiring the gun Zach had lent him. She touched his shoulder. "Are you ready to go to Eudaiz?"

He looked at her. She had never had a chance to look at his deep blue eyes so close. She had always thought he was too beautiful for his temple guard position. But now it turned out he was minor god, and that explained many things.

"I have business to finish, Mya."

"Sure, but we'll come back for that."

"We?"

"Yes, we. I have to go to court. You have to find out about your origin. It seems like our destinies are tangled up with Xiilok and the underworld. I have a feeling this relationship is going to be a long haul."

He nodded. "Are you going to tell me about Kirra?"

"She's part of the long haul matter. So I can't...you'll have to find out for yourself."

He smiled. She knew Leon liked challenges.

Ciaran and Zach approached. "We're all set. Are you ready?" Zach asked.

"It normally doesn't take long at all to teleport back and forth between Eudaiz and Earth. But since you're both first-timers, we have some organization to do," Ciaran said.

"Is there anything we can do to help?" Mya asked.

Ciaran said, "Yes. Before I came, I was having a disagreement with my wife..."

Zach laughed. "The king and his first councillor having a spat!"

"It's not funny, Zach."

"I've known Madeline for ten years. She wouldn't disagree with you for no reason. If you need a vote, you won't get mine." Zach grinned.

"I'm not asking for your vote. I'm asking Mya and Leon to support me."

"I'm good with a fight if you need me," Leon said.

"What is this, Ciaran?" Mya asked.

"Well, it has been a very tough coronation process to get the government in Eudaiz in order. I think we have momentum. Given that our top enemy has run off to Xiilok, I'd like to pursue him instantly before he can gain any ground."

"You want to attack Xiilok right away?" Zach asked.

"That sounds reasonable," Leon said.

"Madeline didn't think you were ready for another fight, I'd guess," Mya said.

"No, it's not me. She's the one who's not ready," Ciaran said.

"Of course she's not ready for you to engage in another battle. How many times did you almost die during the coronation fight? And you almost died twice during this trip. I feel for Madeline, Ciaran," Zach said.

"She took the children." It was Jake's voice.

"What?" Ciaran looked around to find Jake.

"Your microphone is on, Zach," Jake said.

Zach chuckled and was about to turn the microphone off when Jake continued. "Madeline just called. She has brought the children home and would like to talk to you, Ciaran."

"Sure," Ciaran said instantly then cleared his throat. "Of course. Could you please connect the call, Jake?"

"Yes, sir."

Ciaran's face looked as if it was on fire.

"She took the kids! It must have been a hell of a spat, Ciaran. She must really object to you attacking Xiilok now," Zach said.

"But it's not just Xiilok now," Ciaran said. "It's the Babylonian court, the underworld, the gods and goddesses—all of their affairs are entangled. Hoyt is the nastiest sorcerer you could ever come across. And he knows technology well. If he ever gets into bed with one of those forces we just dealt with, we'll be in deep trouble. We have to preempt that."

"I agree," Leon said.

Mya said, "All right, how about this? We get to Eudaiz and let things settle a bit. We attend the underworld court to see how Ishtar's affairs turn out and how many connections she had with Xiilok and other worlds. Then we can figure out how much it has to do with Eudaiz's current situation, and after that, we can decide on the attack."

Ciaran said, "So can I have your word that if it's proven that the Xiilok matter has to be dealt with urgently, you will support me on this decision?"

"Sure," Zach said.

"I'm in," Mya said.

Leon shrugged. "Sure. But I wouldn't mind some battle scars..."

Ciaran looked down at his shirtless body. "Oh hell! Jake, can you pause the call?"

"No, sir, it has already been engaged."

"What's the matter?" Zach asked.

Ciaran pointed to the still swollen red scar on his left shoulder, the scar the tree branch had made. Because the injury was serious and close to his eudqi point, it would take a long time to heal. "One look at this and she'll know how close I was—"

"To being killed?" Zach said. "And you don't think she'd see it tonight when you get back?"

"I need time. I can explain it to her. But now is not the right time. I need to cover up..." Ciaran looked around. "Give me your shirt, Zach."

"My loyalty to you doesn't stretch that far, Ciaran."

"Okay, I'll fix this," Mya said and switched on her deity mode. She ran like wind into town and grabbed two shirts at a shop. But when she reached into her pocket for money, she couldn't find the tiny wallet she always carried with her. *Damn.* She turned around and ran away with the shirts. "I'm so sorry," she yelled as she ran away. "I'll come back and pay you. But not now!"

She charged to the top of the hill and tossed the shirts to Ciaran and Leon. Ciaran slid into the shirt just as the holocast flashed open.

The image of Madeline appeared. Mya had seen her from a distance when she was on a job in London but never up close. Madeline was compelling. That was the only way to describe her.

And in front of her astonished eyes stood Ciaran, king of a universe, the most powerful and knowledgeable creature in the cosmos, shoving his hands nervously into his pant pockets and looking up at his wife's image with unwavering love in his eyes. Just a second ago, he had been strategizing and plotting for votes to go on a battle. But now, he was only a man in love.

She didn't know a tear had rolled down her face until Zach pulled her into his arms and wiped it off. Then he kissed her.

Then they heard Madeline laugh. Mya turned around and looked. Madeline couldn't help but laugh at Ciaran, who was now looking down at his shirt. He turned around. The shirt she had stolen for him was a black T-shirt she thought would complement his fair skin, striking eyes, and thick, long black hair. But on the front of the shirt was a large image of a koala hugging a pink heart and text reading "I Love Wagga Wagga."

Zach pulled Mya into his arms and held her. "She's under my protection, pal," he said to Ciaran.

End of book 2

THE MULTIVERSE COLLECTION
BY D.N. LEO
READING ORDER
http://dnleo.com

A SHADE OF MIND
The Journey from Earth to Eudaiz

Main Characters: Ciaran, Madeline, Tadgh, and Jo
(Recommended reading in order)
1-4 Random Psychic
2-4 Forever Mortal
3-4 Elusive Beings
4-4 Imperfect Divine

MINDSCAPE

Main characters:
Ciaran, Madeline, Tadgh, Jo, Kyle, Hoyt, Ayana, Pete,
Sizx, Lorcan, Orla
(Recommended reading in order within series, can be
read in ANY order in related to other series)

Mindscape One
1-6 Queen's Gambit
2-6- Knight & Pawn

Mindscape Two
3-6 Lone Castle
4-6 Doubled Bishops

Mindscape Three
5-6 Dead Squares
6-6 King's Endgame

—

SPECTRUM

Main characters: Lorcan, Orla, Roy and Mori
(Recommended reading in order)
1-4 White Curse
2-4 Blue Fox
3-4 Indigo Stone
4-4 Red Moon

—

THE GOOD DEITY

Main characters:
Zach, Mya, Leon, Kirra, Dex, Ciaran

Almost Countable
Almost Sure
Almost Everywhere

DARK SOLAR
Main characters:
Dinah, Arik, Ciaran, Madeline, Zach

Three Square

Four Square
Five Square

SILVER BLOOD

Main characters:
Ciaran, Madeline, Tadgh, Jo, Caedmon, Sedna, Roy,
Mori, Zach, Mya, Lorcan and Orla
This series can be read in ANY order within the series
and in related to other series.

Virgo
Libra
Scorpio

Thank you for reading.

If you enjoyed reading **The Good Deity - Book 2**, I would appreciate it if you would help others enjoy this book, too.

Recommend it. Please help other readers find this book by recommending it to friends, readers' groups and discussion boards.

Review it. Please tell other readers why you liked this book by reviewing it. A few sentences will make a significant difference to me. If you do write a review, please send me an email at info@dnleo.com so I can thank you with a personal email.

Connect with me online:
Web: http://dnleo.com ; Twitter: @dnleostory

Facebook
https://www.facebook.com/dnleomultiverse/

COPYRIGHT

ALMOST SURE
The Good Deity - Book 2

By D.N. Leo